Soul Of A Man

Jamie Begley

Soul Of A Man

ISBN-13: 978-0615905198
ISBN-10: 0615905196

Prologue

Fate stood in the corner, invisible to the three adults entering the room filled with children of varying ages. A couple seeking to adopt a child and the social worker eager to find a good home for one of her charges. Fate's lip curled into a sneer, *some loving home*. The woman seeking to adopt would be no loving mother, but a monster in hiding. Her weak husband knew the evil she hid, yet he sought to appease the monster and turn her viciousness toward a new victim.

"How old is this one?" Susan Greer stood over a small, delicate blond girl.

The social worker looked at her notes. "She is seven-years-old."

Fate waved her hand. Susan Greer frowned. "Too old." She moved toward a boy with brown hair quietly playing with blocks on a small table.

"This one?" she questioned.

"Ten." The social worker began to tell her about the boy, "Sam is a quiet child. He loves attention and is quite affectionate." Fate again waved her hand.

"Again, too old. Don't you have any that are younger?"

Noticing the frown beginning to form on the social worker's face, Susan Greer—a master manipulator— forced an insincere smile to her lips. "I just believe the adjustment will be much easier for a younger child."

"I see." Looking at her notes, she walked to a dark haired boy who was trying desperately to hide behind a toy box.

"This young man is Jericho; he is four-years-old. His father is deceased and his mother recently signed over parental rights. She has a drug addiction and could no longer take care of him. Children services had been called in for neglect."

"How sad." Susan reached down to touch the boy, but he shrank back further against the wall. "Would you like to come home with us?"

A mutinous pair of dark eyes stared back at the woman. "No! I don't wanna go." He turned toward the social worker pleadingly. "Please, I don't wanna go with the mean lady."

"Now, Jericho, this nice lady and her husband want to adopt you and make a nice home for you. Wouldn't you like a bedroom to yourself?"

"No!"

"He's the one. I can tell he desperately needs us. Don't you agree, Frank?"

"Whatever you want, dear." Susan Greer turned her beady eyes towards her husband, who began to visibly shake with her attention turned to him.

"Fine, let's go to the office. Your paperwork has already been approved by the State. We'll set up a visitation schedule and a home visit when Jericho knows you better." The social worker was excited by the prospect of a potential adoption. There were so many children to place and too few people willing to adopt. Any doubts she personally had about the Greer's she suppressed. After all, the State had approved their application after a thorough background check. With over a hundred children to supervise, she was too busy to second guess the State's decision.

"That sounds wonderful. I can't wait until we're one, big, happy family." She stared down at the little boy who stared back at her with eyes that seemed to see the evil inside her. She couldn't wait until his training would begin. She bent down to the small boy.

"I'll be seeing you soon, my dear." As they left the room, Jericho knew the scary woman would be back for him.

Fate watched the boy as he bravely fought his frightened tears, his trembling lips firmed, and she barely heard his whispered words, "She don't scare me." She stiffened when she realized he had spoken directly to her.

Fate was invisible to human eyes, yet the child could see her.

"Sometimes my job just sucks!" Fate muttered before she disappeared.

Chapter One

The crowd was huge. Fate frowned; her sister should have arrived at the meeting before her. She supposed she could brave Mother Nature and Father Time alone, however she preferred to wait until she had reinforcements. Mother was going to be angry with her for not bringing her daughters, and it was never a good thing to piss off Mother.

Taking a drink from a passing cherub, Fate could only guess whose bright idea that had been to have them as servers; probably using them to soothe over any discord arising from within the room. Not that they would be much help, without their powers they were useless. Then again, so was everyone else in the room of immortals.

To gain entrance to the high council meeting all immortals' powers were removed, courtesy of Merlin's spell, only to be returned upon leaving. This had come about due to the high number of deaths at the first few meetings. You couldn't expect to fill a room with Gods, Saints and Magick, and not expect a little bloodshed. It was only when a vampire had dared to bite Venus that Merlin had come up with a spell, figuratively checking their powers at the door.

It had taken several meetings before the immortals returned to council, wary of trusting Merlin, but there were disputes and wars to settle; personal goals could be accomplished with the council's help. Wars could be shortened and often prevented with the council's guidance and none of the immortals wanted to make the council members irritated at their absence. The council was the best of the best. No one wanted to make them angry. It often had nasty consequences.

Mother Nature and Father Time were co-chairmen, Jupiter represented the Gods, Merlin represented Magick, Christopher represented the Saints and Vlad represented the Earth Spirits. Each could bring prosperity or an extremely painful death.

Fate sighed, these meetings could be quite boring and she had only attended to please Mother Nature. Friends from the beginning of time, they saw little of each of other as their duties required constant vigilance. Mother was looking forward to seeing Zerina, Broni and Cara, but Fate had been unable to bring herself to allow them to leave home. She consoled her own guilty conscience that they were busy and it would have been too dangerous to leave mortals unattended during the meetings, though Fate knew it was a weak argument and wouldn't cut it with Mother. Friends they may be, yet Fate was expected to obey her demands.

"Why the frown?" Fate turned toward her sister's voice.

"You're late." Destiny shrugged.

"I had a last minute assignment. You don't seem too pleased, what's wrong?"

"Just bored, I guess." Fate tried to shrug off the feeling of impending doom; it was never a good thing for her to feel this way.

"Perhaps we should leave?" Destiny turned and headed for the door.

"No, I've yet to speak to Mother Nature and Father Time. I have to stay until the vote on Rocque comes from the council."

"He doesn't look too worried," Destiny muttered.

Fate shrugged. "He has repeatedly warned others to stay out of his forest. His wolves were attacked and slaughtered by the rogue vampires. He dealt with them far kinder than Vlad would have."

Destiny stared at her sister in disbelief. "He burnt them at a huge bonfire during daylight. That's overkill don't you think?"

"Vlad would have tortured them first. You're just mad because he doesn't fear you."

"That only proves his stupidity." Destiny looked at the arrogant Lord. His day was coming.

Her thoughts were captured by her sister's laughter.

"Relax. This is supposed to be our time of freedom from our responsibilities."

"One day he will go too far," Destiny muttered.

"Don't worry; I think I can guarantee a front row seat." Fate laughed, finally allowing herself to relax for the first time since her arrival.

"Promise me?" Destiny laughed, looking forward to her sister's interference, mischief plain on her striking face.

"I promise," Fate answered. "Look, the council is returning with a verdict." They listened quietly as Mother read off Rocque's punishment.

Destiny turned away in disappointment. "I can't believe it."

"I can. He's one of Mother's favorites. Come on; let's go see our dear friend so I can get out of here."

As the two women made their way forward, many turned to watch their progress. Everyone in the room feared them to some extent. They were the Moirae, feared by all. Conversations lowered and ceased, not wanting themselves heard. Many stared as the women passed with their white gowns hugging their bodies, their creamy skin and dark hair striking. Some even scampered out of their way, not wanting to be noticed.

"I see Aphrodite is with Valentine."

"Slut," Destiny retorted.

"Venus is flirting with Vlad."

"Bitch."

"Morgana La Faye and Merlin are arguing over in the corner."

"Psycho."

They were still laughing as they reached Mother Nature's dais where she was talking with Rocque who moved aside at their approach, but didn't leave as both had hoped. Bowing, they waited for their nod of permission before rising.

"Daughters." Mother's eyes searched the crowd.

"Mother, you are looking beautiful as usual."

"Where are your daughters?" Mother Nature turned her icy glare toward her disobedient subject. "It was my wish that they come."

"They have their duties—" Fate began before being rudely cut off.

"Cut the crap, Fate. We all have important duties. You refused to bring them because you want them kept at home under your thumb." Fate stiffened at her friend's censure.

"That's not true. They leave the safety of our home frequently, but—"

"Be quiet! We both know that you did not bring them because you try to hide them away from the other immortals. Their beauty is well known. You try to hide them for no reason. You of all should know this."

"They are still young, needing guidance—" Fate again was interrupted.

Mother's eyes narrowed. "Your daughters are centuries old. Beware Fate, the arrogance which you and your sister are so quick to judge others of could be your downfall."

"Are you warning me, Mother?" Fate became rigid at

Mother's harsh words.

Mother Nature sighed. "Fate, you and Destiny are headed for a rude awakening if you do not change your ways. I have spoiled you both, so I must also take responsibility for the way you behave. But I am giving you fair warning, I won't tolerate your disobedience much longer." Mother Nature now included both women in her glare.

"What have I done? I have no children to bring." Destiny smirked at her sister, for once glad she hadn't brought their friend's displeasure down upon their heads.

"And that is another bone of contention with me, Destiny. Your failure to provide me with additional children. You know the world desperately needs your daughters, yet you have failed to do so. May I ask just what you are waiting for?"

"I am not ready to become a wife or a mother." Destiny shrugged.

"Do you know who the father will be?" Mother Nature questioned.

"I do not," Destiny replied. "You know we can not see our own future."

"Yes, but I am beginning to believe you have a suspicion of who he is."

Destiny shrugged again, not quite meeting Mother's eyes. "He is immortal, I am an immortal. There is plenty of time."

Mother Nature grew rigid in fury. "You dare to be glib with me?" Destiny knew when she had gone too far.

"I apologize, Mother. I didn't mean to sound glib."

"Daughter, do not apologize to me unless you mean it. Be very careful, Destiny, there is one who wants you bad enough to not fear you or your sister's powers."

Fear glinted briefly in Destiny's eyes before she quickly hid it behind her usual sarcasm.

"I can't believe anyone is that stupid."

"Neither can I," a snide voice said.

Destiny turned toward Rocque. "This is a private conversation; move along, Spot."

Ice dripped from Rocque's voice. "What did you call me?"

"I'm sorry; did I misunderstand your punishment? Aren't you sentenced to being a dog for the next decade?" This was in itself no punishment for an immortal like Rocque. The council could have forced him to become any living object; instead they allowed him to keep the form of a wolf, which he usually ran around in anyway.

"Wolf; not a dog, a wolf." Rocque became angrier at Destiny's sarcastic smile.

"Ah, my mistake, a wolf." She turned around, giving him her back, not seeing the reaction her final retort produced. "Perhaps the bitches you enjoy rutting on will keep you from messing in matters that are not your concern."

"All matters of the Forest are my concern." Rocque's hands clenched into fists.

Destiny turned back to face the angry Lord. "I thought that was the council's job, not yours."

"I merely intervened."

"You interfered," Destiny corrected him.

Rocque shrugged his broad shoulders. "It won't be the last time."

"Want to bet?" Destiny raised her hands, determined to zap the hell out of him. Rocque's laughter stopped their motion.

"You're powerless here, remember?" Destiny fumed at his sarcastic words.

"Be careful, Rocque, that you don't make me angry. I could always have you mate with one of your bitches at an opportune time to ensure fertility. I think a father of sextuplets would cramp your style quite a bit, don't you?" Her laughter rang out when Rocque's face paled at her threat. "Better yet, perhaps I'll introduce you to Morgana La Faye. I think you would make a delightful couple."

Destiny was speechless when Rocque merely gave her a devilish smile. "If you're giving out introductions, why not introduce me to your three nieces? I could be persuaded to take one to wife." Seeing Destiny beginning to shake in fury, Rocque's satisfaction at riling her became evident. "We'll be one, big, happy family. That would make you my aunt."

Destiny's temper exploded. She leapt at him, determined to knock the arrogant smirk off his face, however, before she could make contact, Odin caught her in mid-air. "Calm yourself, Destiny."

Destiny pointed her finger at Rocque. "You will never have one of my nieces. That, I can guarantee."

Rocque was cut short when he began to make another reply. "Be quiet, Rocque!" Odin bellowed over Destiny's shrieks of anger.

"Let her go."

Odin turned with Destiny still in his arms at Fate's order. "Control your sister." Odin released Destiny from his hold.

Fate snapped at the God. "Destiny will stop when Lord Doggie quits aggravating her, and she is quite right, he will never have one of my daughters." Seeing Rocque tense at Fate's words, and about to start an argument with her, Odin coldly took control.

"Fate, you and your sister cannot continue trying to intimidate others with your powers."

"I don't know why not." Fate gave a delicate shrug. "Destiny gives them a fair chance. She gives them a choice. I merely step in when it's made."

"And you of course have never made a mistake?" Odin questioned.

"Oh, I have made several." Her eyes slid toward Valentine then returned to Odin's. "Some worse than others." Her disgust of him plain on her face.

Odin's muscled frame stiffened as anger filled his rugged features. "You dare talk to me with such disrespect?"

"Yes, I dare! I have every right to be furious with you. You tricked me into believing you were Valentine!" Fate yelled at the God, not caring that everyone in the room was listening.

"Fate, you knew within minutes it was me. You simply chose to pretend it was him."

"I did not, though I should have. He is much better in bed."

At her snide remark, Odin took a step toward her, determined to throttle her.

"I'll show you who's better—"

Fate took a step forward, not afraid of the pissed off God. "You will never touch me again. Dare and I will pay Merlin to turn your dick into a dried up fig, you old…"

All the eyes in the room spun toward Merlin, who turned pale at Odin's glare. "I would never." He squeaked at the thought of Odin's fury turned toward him. Terror was obvious on the old magician's lined face.

"Enough!" screamed Mother Nature, her crown slipping sideways on her head at the same time her raised voice woke Chronas, who had been napping in the chair at her side, oblivious to the arguments going on around him. With a jeweled hand, she righted her golden crown while also giving the sisters a reprimanding stare.

"I see why you two don't have husbands. Who could put up with you hellions for an eternity?" Both women unrepentantly nodded their heads in agreement.

"You both seek to escape that which you cannot control." She shook her head at her wayward subjects. Before they could interrupt, she raised her hand and continued. Sadness shone out of her eyes as her voice gentled. They were her favorites of all the immortals, but their obvious insubordination could no longer be ignored. Fate and Destiny gave each other worried looks, Mother rarely—if ever—showed her gentle side. "You both are quick to determine other's futures, but run from your own.

Fate, by disobeying me, you have brought about yours and Destiny's downfall."

"Me?" Fate gasped, "I didn't do anything!"

"Yes, Fate, you did. I repeatedly asked you to bring your daughters. In doing so, you would have protected them tonight. Instead, they were left vulnerable to attack. I gave you that which you say so often you give others, a choice. Your sister already knows this, which is why she was late."

Fate turned toward her sister accusingly. "You betrayed me," Fate whispered hoarsely.

"You know I would not." Hurt, Destiny stepped toward her sister. "I repeatedly told you not to disobey Mother, and while there was still time, I tried to get you to leave the council. You know I could only give you the choice. If I had done any more, I would have lost my powers and been unable to help my nieces when they will need me the most."

"I must go." Frantically, Fate headed toward the doorway that would give her back her powers. Perhaps there was still time to fix…

"Fate," Mother's voice rang out across the room, but that wasn't what stopped Fate and had her turning around to face her. It wasn't her friend and confidant of centuries she faced now, but the chairman of the council.

"You cannot interfere; what has begun cannot be stopped. If you try to intervene, you will lose your powers." At her obvious pain, Mother's voice softened, "Fate, you must learn as other mothers before you have learned. You can only protect your children for so long. They have to learn to lead their own lives and make their own mistakes. It is the cycle of life; we cannot interfere."

Fate nodded. "May I please leave now?" Without waiting for a reply, she again turned toward the doorway. Rushing through it, her powers returned fully. Instantly, she knew what had transpired during her absence.

"She'll interfere," Destiny said, unable to hide her fear.

There was no pity on the faces surrounding her. Odin and Rocque were smiling at each other with satisfied smirks. Destiny had a terrible feeling; many had waited for this day to arrive.

"She'll try." Destiny didn't like the look in Mother's eyes, and began trembling when she realized the warning had not been for Fate alone.

Chapter Two

Cara watched the young girl recklessly riding the horse. Adoni was enjoying the freedom she had gained from sneaking away from her mother's watchful eyes. She had been born sickly and it had taken all of Broni's powers to hold her to the life her delicate soul had so often sought to escape. It had not been her time then, however now her time had come. Adoni was fifteen, a young girl just slipping into a womanhood that would never come. That was why Cara was there; she was an escort for souls, leading them to their next life.

Some souls left willingly, eager to leave their bodies, not afraid of the next step. Other's fought leaving, not wanting to leave loved ones or afraid to face the unknown. It was Cara's job to escort them through that doorway, to soothe their fears and provide comfort. Death of their physical bodies was just a new beginning. Cara helped them through their fears.

"Why are you here?" Cara turned at her sister's voice.

"You know why I am here, Broni. It is Adoni's time."

"No, there is still time to save her." Cara was already shaking her head.

"You can not prevent this, Broni. You cannot save her. The time and place of her death cannot be changed." Cara reached out to take her sister's trembling hand. "You have fought and protected her as long as possible, now you must step aside and let me help her this last time." The tears on Broni's face tore at Cara's heart. Just once Cara wished she could change fate. Save a soul from death and return empty handed to the doorway to the afterlife. Cara knew it could never happen; she was only called when death was a foregone conclusion.

Their attention was caught as the horse broke stride and stumbled, sending Adoni flying through the air, landing roughly on the hard ground. Without a thought, both women were instantly by her side. Broni reached out to smooth her hair away from her glazed eyes. Adoni could not see either woman, she just felt a comforting presence while the initial fear and pain she felt began easing away. Cara knew all her thoughts and emotions and sent a surge of comfort to the child's broken body.

"Please don't let her suffer," Broni begged Cara.

Cara soothed Broni, "You know I would not."

Broni looked at her delicate sister. Her appearance alone would provide comfort. Her long, black hair, blue eyes, and an air of frailty led one to believe they were seeing an angel. They probably were; Cara was as beautiful on the inside as she was on the outside. Her inner beauty giving her a gentleness and purity of spirit that Broni had seen in no other. Broni and Zerina had often said that even angels were jealous of her beauty. They had often wondered if that was why their mother had hidden them away. Had she been afraid of some of the Goddess's— such as Hera, Venus and Aphrodite's—petty jealousies? Broni shrugged her shoulders, who knew why their mother did the things she did?

Cara's physical appearance became ethereal as Adoni's spirit joined her. Broni could not see Adoni, only Cara could see a soul before they crossed through the doorway to the afterlife. Broni looked at the lifeless body and could no longer hold back her tears. Adoni had held a special place in her heart; she had fought many battles on her behalf.

Cara felt her other sister's presence mere seconds before her arrival. Zerina always knew when one of her sisters needed her. When Broni felt her sister's touch, she turned into her warm embrace.

"Broni, you know that you will see her again," Zerina comforted.

Broni nodded. "I don't know why I'm crying."

"Because your part in her life is at an end. She no longer needs you to fight for her, and that is hard for you. I feel your sadness, I was part of her birth, saw life enter her, and it was with sadness that I saw this happening, but we can do no other than assist. We cannot interfere."

Both women watched as Cara spoke to the little spirit, though neither could hear her words. Zerina made an offer she had never made before.

"Would you like to help escort her?"

"How is that possible?" Broni questioned.

"With Cara's help we can travel with her to the doorway. Mother is at the council, she would not know until her return." Broni smiled. Zerina was always trying to please those she loved. She was the most powerful of the three, often not able to show emotion at the decisions her job demanded.

Her gift was to find the right spirit for their physical forms. Present at the birth of each child, she often had to make decisions that Broni did not know if she could make. Especially if the soul was entering into a home where it would not be properly loved or cared for. Zerina often said those required stronger souls because they had to survive despite those hardships.

Cara turned and held out her hand to her. Broni reached out and took it, instantly becoming ethereal. She then realized Zerina was holding her other hand. Linked, they were now able to see Adoni's spirit.

"Are you angels, too?"

"We are not angels, we are Moriae."

"Moriae?" Adoni questioned.

"We are your guides through life. Zerina was with you at your birth, Broni helped and protected you through your physical life, and I am Cara. I am here to help you to your new afterlife."

"Am I being punished for disobeying my mother? She told me I was never to ride alone, but it was such a beautiful day, I could not resist."

"It had nothing to do with you disobeying your mother. It is time for your beautiful spirit to move forward to a new life. Do you remember when you and you mother moved to a new village? How frightened you were? How much you came to love your new home?"

"Yes, but my mother was there," Adoni whispered.

"Your mother can not be with you yet, it is not her time. When it is, you can greet her, she will not be as frightened, and you will be able to introduce her to all your new friends. But this time you must be brave on your own, Adoni. I promise you have nothing to fear." Cara read her thoughts. "Broni will look out for your mother, as she has protected you."

Broni spoke up, "I have been by your side during your many illnesses. The night that you escaped the fire that burned down your home, I made sure you awakened in time to escape. I give you my word, I will protect your mother."

Reassured, Adoni turned to Cara. "I'm ready."

Cara and the others slowly began to slip away, carried away in what seemed like rushing wind, but was not. Movement became nothing more than a moment in time until it seemed as if they were walking in the sky itself with bright stars surrounding the three women.

Broni understood now why souls could become lost. There were so many directions and bright lights glittering in the darkness. The vastness of it all would have been overwhelming without Cara's help. Without hesitation, she guided them through the darkness, leading them to a destination that only Cara knew. Adoni suddenly tried to break free and move toward one particularly bright light, but Cara tightened her grip on the girl, moving her forward.

"That doorway is not yours, Adoni."

"But I want to go there; it's so beautiful." Adoni became petulant. Being young, she was attracted to the beautiful doorway.

"It is, but yours is just as beautiful." Cara inexorably moved the girl forward. It was as if there was a path only she could see.

Suddenly a bright light was before them. Cara stopped before they came within touching distance, mere inches away.

"It's not as large as the other one." Disappointment and fear were the emotions Cara sensed within Adoni as well as something Cara couldn't quite put her finger on.

"Darling, the size doesn't matter, only what is inside. Your doorway is just different than the other, not better or worse."

Adoni nodded, relieved. "Will I see you again?" Cara turned and looked into the bright light, studying it for several minutes.

"Yes, you will see us again and soon." Cara tried to hide the apprehension she was feeling from the girl, but Zerina and Broni knew something was wrong.

"Go, Adoni. My sisters and I must leave, and I want you safe before we go."

Zerina and Broni began to feel a disturbance around them. Broni's instincts to protect Adoni again flared within her, but she was unable to move. Holding each sister by the hand; if she released Cara, her and Zerina would be lost in the dark maze, but if she released Zerina, then she would be lost alone.

Cara pushed Adoni toward the light, and as soon as she entered the light, she disappeared.

Cara turned toward her sisters. Clasping Broni's hand tighter, she hurried through the darkness. "Do you feel the disturbance?" Cara spoke quietly.

"Yes, we must hurry, Cara. Someone is following us." Broni kept her voice firm, not wanting her sisters to feel her impending sense of doom. Her feelings were never wrong; they had saved more than one soul.

"No one should be here. I am the only one able to follow these paths."

"They are following us, they wish to destroy us." Broni's battle instincts were surging through her body. She wanted to stay and face the approaching enemy, but would not risk her sisters' safety.

"Whatever happens, we can not release hands. You will become lost and disoriented without my help," Cara spoke hurriedly, feeling the danger draw nearer. She was practically running through the corridor. "Can you tell what it is?"

Both women shook their heads as Cara rushed along the unseen path with her sisters desperately trying to keep up.

"We're almost there." Cara could see their doorway just ahead. They each were praying to reach the doorway before whatever danger stalking them struck. They were inches away from the doorway when they were suddenly hit with a power surge, knocking them apart.

Cara heard her sisters' screams at the same time she felt as if she had been struck by a massive fist in her head. Helplessly, she tried to keep from losing consciousness. She knew it was a losing battle, so Cara attempted to simply stay alert long enough to find her sisters. Seeing a movement to her left, she saw Broni flung towards a particularly small and dark doorway. Dread filled Cara at which doorway Broni had unwillingly entered.

Quickly, she tried to find Zerina, she was beginning to

lose hope when Cara saw her struggling to pull herself out of a doorway when she lost her battle and was dragged backwards as if an invisible hand had grabbed her. Cara knew she was in danger and unable to help her sisters now, but at least she knew how to find them.

Cara started crawling along the dark path, but her sisters' doorways were no longer there, vanishing as each entered. With the doorways closed, Cara was unable to follow. She anxiously searched for one that could at least be used to access her way home. She was about to give up hope when she saw a small doorway to her left, but knowing where it led, she was going to pass it, even as she felt herself grow weaker. There was one further away that held the possibility of being able to follow Zerina.

Crawling on her hands and knees, she was about to pass the small doorway when she heard a voice calling to her. Turning to look in the doorway, she feared she was wasting precious time, barely able to focus, but she heard her name called again. One of her gifts was to be able to see inside each doorway, and unless she was mistaken, that was her aunt Destiny calling for her.

Swiftly changing directions, she began crawling toward the doorway in which she saw her aunt standing. Of all the doorways, Cara would have chosen this doorway last. It would provide many difficulties that would be hard to overcome. Cara barely made it through before she lost consciousness, sensing the doorway closing behind her.

Cara hoped Destiny knew what she was doing leading her here, but doubted she would have made it much further. At least she knew where she was, having visited here many times.

Pain burst behind her eyes and Cara, for the first time, realized what many of her souls felt at their death. However, no one was there to help her, to show her the way home.

* * *

Fate stood on the balcony of her Palace, staring at the

sky before her.

Destiny walked to her sister's side. "Have you found them?"

Tears streaked down her cheeks. "They are mortal."

Destiny also stared at the dark sky, reading the same twinkling lights Fate was observing. "Only a God can retrieve them now. We have so many enemies it will not be safe to send anyone after them."

"There is one," Fate's voice broke. "He hates me, but he will not betray them."

Fate turned back toward the star-studded sky and began weaving a pattern. Twinkling lights moved, slowly adjusting positions, circling a small light that was barely visible.

Destiny reached out and grabbed the arm closest to her. "What are you doing? You cannot interfere."

Fate roughly pulled her arm out of her sister's reach, resuming her weaving. "I am not interfering, I'm assisting. Cara needs help immediately; she took the worst of it trying to protect her sisters."

Destiny watched the pattern Fate spun. A gasp escaped when she finished, turning pale when she saw what Fate had maneuvered.

"You are sending him to help her? Are you crazy?" Destiny could not believe what her own eyes were telling her.

"No one else can protect her as well. He will keep her safe until we can retrieve her."

"He will not help her, he will destroy her! Do not do this, Fate. It is too dangerous."

Angrily, Fate snarled at her sister. "Why did you lead her to that doorway?"

Destiny took a step back from her sister. "She couldn't make it further…"

Fate was so angry she shook. "Just as I now have no choice? He is the only one strong enough to protect her. Hopefully, we can get her from him before he does too much damage." Fate took a last look at the sky and saw that things were going accordingly before she turned and headed back inside the Palace.

"Where are you going now?" Destiny questioned.

Fate answered without turning back, "Where I swore I would never go again. To see Odin, but first I plan to change."

Destiny followed Fate up the marble staircase to her room, watching her change her gown—always white—to another shearer one. The lowered neckline showed much more than a glimpse of her breasts; it barely covered them. Her red nipples were clearly visible through the shear fabric. The gown hugged her figure tightly, showing her still firm stomach and flaring hips. It also provided a hint of the vee between her thighs and her long, trim legs. Diamond-studded sandals flashed as she moved around her room.

"Out to impress?" Destiny stared in amusement.

Fate shrugged. "I want you to go to Cara. Watch out for her, help when you can."

Destiny nodded. "Broni and Zerina?"

"I have already sent others to help them. They are in danger, but not as immediate as Cara."

"Who did you send?" Something told her she didn't want to know, especially when Fate's face turned red. She didn't look her in the eyes, giving Destiny a feeling she wasn't going to like her sister's answer.

"Valentine will be assisting Broni."

"Who are you sending to Zerina?" Destiny didn't try to keep the suspicion out of her voice.

"Jinx."

"Now I know you have lost your mind. Valentine I can understand, he's their father, but Jinx? She's more likely to get Zerina killed than help her."

"I have to take that chance." Fate brushed out her dark hair, leaving it loose. Odin liked it that way. She planned to use every asset she had to get Odin to help. The stubborn

God could not be pushed to lend his help, but maybe he could be seduced.

Chapter Three

"Come on, I need a beer. Tomorrow is our last day on this job, so let's celebrate," Billy wheedled.

The three other men in the cramped hotel room looked at the young man as if he had lost his mind.

"We're beat, kid. We all have a few years on you; it's been a long job." The men all looked like they had been through a war zone. They had just constructed a building, which should have taken over a year to build, within seven months. Each had worked their ass off to reach their bonus if they completed the job early. They had worked together before on many construction jobs and got along well together.

"Jericho, how about you?" Billy turned to the man lying sprawled on his bed, having just taken a shower.

"I'm out for the night. You'll find nothing in their local bar except trouble. Besides, I'm headed home after they give our pay. I have a long drive ahead of me. Being half asleep and nursing a hangover is just asking for trouble."

"Ohio?"

"No thanks, kid." The oldest member of the team was often the most ready to head out for a cold beer. The fact that he said no in itself spoke of the men's weariness.

"Well, I guess I'm on my own. See you guys later." Billy left the room whistling.

The next morning the men were drinking their morning coffee, impatient for the last of the inspectors to finish. Barring any failures, the men would all be paid. Personal vehicles were already loaded and gassed, ready to head out to their various homes. Jericho watched the men talk as he walked with the inspectors. This part always clenched his gut. Sometimes you got some real assholes who only liked the aggravation failing an inspection could cause; others were just looking to get their palms greased for the passing sticker.

The inspector bent and pulled a wire. "The cover's not right." Jericho saw the official looking at the men hanging around and trying to estimate how much he could get for holding the job up.

Jericho didn't argue. "Yes, it is. We passed two other inspections in this state with the same electrical cover."

The inspector started to argue—money flashing through his mind along with the weekend getaway with his girlfriend that a bribe would buy—right up until the moment he looked into Jericho's eyes. He didn't just take a step back, he took two. He had been around a lot of roughneck's during his work, however none had ever made his blood run cold. You didn't have to ponder why he was foreman of the job and how he had kept over a hundred men under his control to get a job of this magnitude done without incident and on time. He was a mean son of a bitch. His palms weren't going to get greased with a bribe; this man was more likely to cut them off first.

Shaking, he bent down to give the cover another cursory look. "It will do." He hurriedly started writing on his clipboard and then handed Jericho the green sticker showing the inspection had passed before walking quickly to his car. The sooner he got away from him, the better for his health.

Jericho walked over to the men waiting. "It's a go. Start lining up and I'll hand out the pay." He frowned as he turned toward the onsite office, noticing a missing truck. "Where's Billy?"

Ohio shrugged. "He never returned to the room last night or this morning before we left."

Rick laughed. "Maybe he got lucky."

Ohio laughed, too. "It would be a first."

"I agree. Rick, drive over to that bar he went to last night and see if you can find out where the kid is."

"Ah, Jericho, Billy can take care of himself. I want to get home."

"Not a man leaves town until we find Billy. We came into this town together and we'll leave together."

No one argued with him as Jericho headed to the office. His desk was by a window so that his eyes were constantly on the site. He had passed out several of the men's pay when he saw Billy's truck drive onto the site, parking next to Jericho's own truck. When Billy emerged, Ohio immediately lit into the kid. Jericho heard the yelling in his office.

"I'm sorry I'm late. I had a flat." Billy couldn't hide his guilty expression.

"Boy, if you got laid and overslept, just say so. You don't have to make up excuses to me. I'm not your mama."

Billy turned bright red and shook his head.

"You better get to the office. Jericho's been looking for you."

Billy got in line with the rest of the crew. When his turn came, he couldn't look Jericho in the eyes.

"Sorry I'm late, boss."

Jericho nodded. "Since you're the last one in, you can do clean up duty."

"But, Jericho, I really need to get out of town. I mean, I need to head home."

Jericho studied the young man. His instincts were telling him that Billy was hiding something, but as long as it didn't involve the job, it was none of his business. There was no quicker way to lose a good crewmember than to stick his nose where it didn't belong.

"You know the rules; last one in does cleanup." Billy nodded. Once Jericho gave an order, he expected the job carried out.

"Hurry up, kid." Jericho watched as Billy left the office and began picking up trash around the site. There wasn't much as Jericho expected the men to pick up after themselves.

After Jericho paid the last of the men, he did a final walk-through of the building. It was his responsibility to check to make sure all the windows and doors in the building were locked.

He was walking out of the building when four police cars pulled onto the lot.

Jericho tensed. This was not a good sign. When the police sent out four squad cars, you could bet that it was going to be a major fuck up.

Billy caught his attention. He looked like a deer caught under a hunter's shotgun. Billy, seeing Jericho's hard stare, bent and kept picking up the trash, hoping to go unnoticed by the police while the other men were loading their tools into vehicles, anxious to head out.

With an experienced eye, Jericho studied the officers as they got out of their cars. He picked out the one with the most pompous attitude. "Can I help you, Sheriff?"

"Who's in charge?" Giving him a narrowed look, which Jericho bet was practiced in front of a mirror, the officer set out to intimidate. It wasn't going to work. Jericho had little left to fear in life, and this asshole wasn't one of them.

"That would be me." Jericho stared each man in the eyes, knowing that to look scared was like feeding raw meat to hungry sharks. "Can I help you?" Again, Jericho repeated his question.

"We have a report of a missing woman who escaped from the mental facility twenty miles from here."

"If she's on foot, then why would you think she would be here? We haven't seen a woman hanging around. Believe me, my men would have noticed." The few men who had stepped closer to overhear the conversation started catcalling and whistling.

"Shut up!" one of the officers yelled at the men.

"They're just letting off some steam. A lot of them have been away from home for a while." Jericho's tone warned he wouldn't let the men be harassed for no reason.

The officer stuck out his chest, which only emphasized his paunch.

"One of your men was seen with the woman last night." Jericho didn't have to ask who, but the officer told him anyway.

"The manager at the Stop and Go identified him as a Billy Smith and that he works for this construction crew."

"He does." Jericho cursed to himself. The crew often stopped at the convenience store to grab a coffee or a quick snack.

"Is he here?"

Before Jericho could say anything, Billy spoke up, "I'm here." He walked to stand in front of the officer. The sheriff smiled, showing his shark teeth. Here was a man he could intimidate.

"Did you see this young woman?" The Sheriff produced a picture from the folder he was holding.

"I talked to a lot of women last night." Billy tried to smile when the men standing around started to cheer again. When Jericho saw the officers getting angry, he motioned the men away.

"Long, dark hair, blue eyes and a white dress." Even Jericho could see Billy had seen the woman. He couldn't hide the guilty look in his eyes.

"I gave her a ride to the Stop and Go last night when I

left the bar."

"Mind if we check out your truck?"

Jericho spoke up, "Got a warrant?"

Another officer handed him the signed warrant. "Show him your truck, Billy."

Billy turned as two officers followed him to his truck. Jericho watched as they searched and then ten minutes later they came back empty-handed.

"Looks like she's not here," Jericho said.

"Mind if we search the site?"

"Help yourself. I've been here all morning, and there's no woman here. You're wasting your time."

"It's mine to waste." The officers spread out and searched the building and storage sheds, even the porta-potties, finding nothing.

"Search the vehicles."

"No. Not unless you have about forty warrants in your possession."

The Sheriff turned to Jericho.

"Why not the vehicles?"

"I have the authorization for you to search the building, but the vehicles are personal property." Jericho knew they wouldn't find the woman, but also knew he managed a rough crew and they probably had a little pot, or an unlicensed weapon. The first he didn't mind if it was done on off time. The weapons were like condoms to some of the men, you never left home without them.

The Sheriff's lips pursed in a smart ass grin. "What did you say your name was?"

"I didn't, but my name is Jericho Hawk."

"And if I pulled your record, what would I find?" Jericho had been down this road many times before. He knew exactly where this conversation was headed.

"That I served two years in prison." Jericho didn't break eye contact.

"What charge?"

"Murder."

"Is that so?"

"I served my time. I'm not even on parole, so you're barking up the wrong tree. The woman is not here."

The Sheriff turned back to the other officers waiting. "Phelps, head over to the courthouse and pick me up some warrants." As he was talking, the scanner could be heard in the background. The Sheriff moved to answer the dispatcher, and within seconds, he was motioning the other officers back to their cars.

"The woman was seen at the Camelot Inn."

"Isn't that just a couple of miles away from the Stop and Go?" Jericho questioned snidely. The asshole Sheriff threw him a dirty look before heading back to his cruiser. "Count yourself lucky that the call came in. I was looking forward to searching your truck personally. Hawk, now that your job is finished, don't stick around town."

Jericho's lips twisted. "Don't worry; I'm gone already." The Sheriff nodded with self importance before getting in his cruiser. The asshole took off, lights flashing and dust flying in all directions.

"Whew, am I glad that's over," Billy tried to joke, but Jericho cut him off.

"I don't want to know what happened last night. I don't care. My best advice is that you get in your truck and haul ass out of this town." Billy nodded and high-tailed it back to his truck and Jericho watched as he as well as the other crewmembers spun out of the parking area.

They were lucky. If that call hadn't come through, they all probably would have been stuck here for several hours, and that was if nothing illegal had been found in the vehicles.

He closed up the site and headed to his own truck. Driving off, he didn't take a last look as the lot disappeared from view. No feeling of satisfaction of a job well done or a thought about the crew crossed his mind while heading home. The job was done and any connection he had to it was over.

As his truck passed the state line, he was just glad to be driving to his own home where he would stay for the next two months. With the bonus money earned on this job, he was due for a rest before the next contract began. He needed it. The last job had been exhausting and major recoup time was needed. The only excitement he was looking for was a clean bed and a warm body next to him.

Jericho was definitely glad to be out of that town. If Billy was smart, he had taken his advice and gotten out also because one thing Jericho had learned in prison was to know when someone was lying, and that kid had been lying, badly. There was no way Jericho would have put his own ass on the line for him, though. He had learned the hard way no bitch was worth doing time.

Chapter Four

Cara huddled under the tarp where every bump and curve the truck took jarred her sore body. Her trembling fingers gripped the bolted down tire to keep herself steady. Cara didn't even know whose truck she was in or where they were going. Thoughts of her sisters' safety were all that kept her thoughts occupied between bumps. Her body was in pain, though, and Cara was unused to the sensation.

It hadn't taken her long to figure out that going through that doorway had made her mortal. She knew her mother was probably furious, but would be unable to help.

She had no idea how long they had been driving before Cara felt the truck come to a stop. Making herself lay still despite her aching body, she felt the truck shake when the door slammed closed. She tried to hear what was going on outside the truck, but couldn't with the tarp muffling any sound. Could they be at their destination? Or just stopping for something else?

Cara was familiar with human's moves, having visited earth many, many times. She was tempted to take a peek from under the tarp, yet she was afraid of being seen. She would wait just a little longer and then, if the man didn't return, she would take a small peek.

Cara hoped that Billy had known what he was doing when he slipped her into the truck when no one was looking. She had heard the men searching the other truck not long after. She simply had to trust the man that had helped her when he had seen her lying unconscious on the side of the road. The young man had sat with her in his truck until she had quit shaking and could gather her strength. It wasn't every day that an immortal become mortal. The cold had been the worst, and her flimsy dress hadn't made it much better.

His gentle soul had listened to her and believed her when she had told him how she had become lost. After he had listened, he had driven her to the local all night store and purchased warmer clothes for her. Cara was now dressed in jeans, a sweatshirt, socks and shoes. Along with the warm coat and gloves, she had finally gained enough warmth to quit shaking. After that, a drive-thru had provided her with food and her first taste of coffee. Thinking back, Cara could almost taste the warm silk as it had slid down her throat for the first time. It hadn't been long before an uncomfortable feeling had her asking for help. With a red face, he had taken her to a small store to use the restroom.

When Billy realized he was late for work, he had hidden her in the back of the truck, explaining that she wouldn't have to be hidden long, and that his friends would ask to many questions that wouldn't be safe to answer. Then, he could take her to his home and help her find her sisters. She had lain quietly until he had raised the tarp, motioning her to be quiet, and had hidden her in the truck next to his. Before he had pulled the tarp over her again, she had noticed several cars pulling into the parking lot. The fear on Billy's face hadn't needed explanations. She had thought that he would come back for her, and only realized when the truck had began moving that he hadn't been able to.

Cara felt the truck shake with the door slamming once again and then she felt the truck moving. The long drive seemed endless.

Cara began dozing. She didn't know how long she had been asleep before she felt herself grabbed and pulled roughly from the truck. Staring up into a furious face, Cara felt herself stifling a scream at the man standing before her. He was definitely no Billy. This man had not an ounce of gentleness or understanding in his body.

"What the hell!" Jericho didn't need to be told that his hidden hitchhiker was the escaped mental patient. His palm slammed against the side of the truck. "Son of a Bitch! I'll kill him."

Cara's frightened gaze took in his fury, and she started to tremble in fear. He was over six feet tall, his tan face and black hair seemed even darker against his grey-eyed stare. His muscles strained as if he had to hold himself in check from striking her.

Before she could open her mouth, his harsh words cut her short, "Get moving."

Without looking at her again, he moved to the back of his truck and started pulling out the wheel she had previously been curled against. She watched as he moved the heavy wheel with little effort and then walked to the side of the truck, sliding it on. Cara saw another already lying on the side with a deep gash. When he was done, he picked up the flat one and threw it and some metal things into the back.

Easily jumping up into the bed, he bolted the damaged tire, placing the metal tools into a metal box, before jumping back down. Cara simply stood there in her new clothes and trembled. She didn't know what to say to this hard man. She had never dealt with one whose soul was so black. Usually it was Grimm who would have been sent out to escort souls such as his.

Cara had not lost all her powers becoming mortal. She could still see the colors of their souls and the loved ones close by that she had escorted to their afterlife standing by them. This man had neither. No one who had loved this man had passed, or he hadn't cared if they had. Even the serial killers had mothers or fathers who had cared. He had no one.

With a last look at her, he walked to his door, got in and drove off without looking back. Cara's mouth hung open. The rude bastard had just left her standing on the side of the road. She looked around and saw they were on a two-lane road with no other cars within sight. Cara didn't know what to do so she merely started walking, not understanding how she had ended up in this predicament.

Who could have the power to enter the Halls of Death? The power surge had been unexpected and supposedly impossible within the passage between worlds. Lost in her thoughts, she stumbled over a rock, but kept walking.

When Cara turned a corner, she saw the truck waiting a few feet up and she quickened her steps before he could change his mind. As scary as he was, it was preferable to being alone. Walking up to the passenger side of the truck, she waited while he maneuvered the window down with a push of a button.

"Get in."

Without hesitation, Cara opened the door and jumped in. The truck spun out as soon as she shut the door. She grabbed the dashboard as she was almost flung off the seat.

"Buckle up." He spoke without glancing at her.

She clasped the seatbelt around her that Billy had showed her how to work the previous night. Cara was beginning to feel like a pro dealing with trucks. It was kind of comforting in this strange world.

"I'll give you a lift to the next gas station, twenty miles from here, and then you're on your own."

Cara nodded. "Thank you." She didn't try to convince him to help her; it would be a wasted effort.

"Why were you in the mental hospital? Did you try to

hurt yourself or someone else? My guess is someone else with the amount of police presence looking for you."

"I wasn't in a mental hospital." Cara felt a chill up her back. She was very familiar with the mental hospitals and nursing homes. Both were a dumping ground for the unwanted in their society.

"Don't lie to me or I'll dump your ass on the side of the road and this time I won't come back."

"I'm not. I was not nor have I ever been a patient at one of those institutions."

"Then suppose you tell me why the police were looking for you."

"I don't know. I did not know anyone in that town other than Billy. I can only think that the one responsible for me being there sent them."

"And that person would be?"

"I don't know."

He turned to look at her with a snarl on his lips. "Listen, cupcake, I'm taking a chance just having you in my truck. If you've committed a crime and I'm caught with you, then they could get me for being an accessory. Now, for the last time, tell me why the police are looking for you."

"I'm not lying. I don't know. I haven't done anything illegal."

"Why were you in Corbin?" he snarled the words between clenched teeth.

"Is that the name of the town?" At his sharp nod, she went on, "Because that is where I was dropped."

"Who dropped you off?"

"I don't know." Jericho could feel his patience straining at her ambiguous answers.

"Let me see if I understand this correctly. You were dropped off in Corbin for no reason by someone you don't know with the police in said town looking to arrest you for no reason that you can think of."

"Yes."

"I ought to put you out here and now, the only reason I don't is because we're almost at the gas station. Is that all you got to tell me?"

"All that you will believe."

He looked at her exasperated. "I don't believe anything you've told me. Can you at least answer one question truthfully?"

"I have answered all your questions truthfully. But yes, I'll answer your question."

"Why are you wearing a winter coat and gloves in eighty degree weather?"

Cara hesitated, but spoke truthfully, "Because my body has not yet adjusted to its new environment."

"New environment?"

Cara nodded her head. "Where I come from bodies do not feel heat or cold. Our body temperatures are constant."

"What are you, an alien or one of the loony's who believe they were abducted then returned by aliens?"

"I am not an alien, nor have I ever met one. I can guarantee they do not exist."

"Not that I'm disagreeing with you or anything, and I'm sincerely grateful that you have no relationship with one, but how can you guarantee that they don't exist. Even scientists don't agree on that one."

"Because I know every creature known and unknown ever created."

"You do? And how is that possible?" Cara didn't miss that his voice had changed its tone as if he was placating a crazy person. Cara didn't appreciate his condescending attitude.

"Because I am a Moraie." Cara's own tone had turned smug. She was very proud of her heritage.

"Exactly what is a Moraie?" Again with the attitude. It was seriously beginning to grate on her nerves.

"Have you ever heard of the three fates?" Looking at him, she guessed he hadn't. "One is present at birth,

37

guiding souls to the correct child's body. That is my sister, Zerina. Another is present during your life, helping to fight battles along the way. The way they are meant to for the good or bad. That is my sister, Broni." The whole time she was talking, Cara noticed his hands tightening on the steering wheel.

"And you?"

"I am the third fate. My name is Cara."

"And what do you do?"

"I cut the thread. I free the soul and escort it to their next life."

"So you're a serial killer?"

Aghast, Cara stared at him. "I am responsible for no one's death. I am only sent for when death is a forgone conclusion."

"Did you explain this crap to Billy?"

"Yes, I did. And at first, he also did not believe me."

"But you were eventually able to convince him?"

"Yes, I was."

"That's not so surprising; he probably took one look at you and would have believed anything you told him." Jericho took in her long, straight, black hair, blue eyes and creamy skin. In her winter coat she looked like a ski bunny. The boy hadn't stood a chance against her looks. He would have been putty in her hands. However Jericho was no boy and he wasn't buying a word that came out of those perfect lips.

"He believed me not only because I spoke the truth, but I had proof."

"Now, you just said something to surprise me. What proof? Show it to me."

"I can't."

"Why not? If you have this proof, why show it to Billy and not me?"

"Because of your soul." At this, his whole body tightened.

"My soul?"

Now Cara spoke carefully, not wanting to anger him, nor did she know if it was even possible to hurt his feelings. She hated hurting people, she had found even the toughest souls had a weak spot and didn't want to cause additional hurt.

"Billy's soul was white, gentle and kind. He also had a mother that had recently passed. She was still close to him. He knew I spoke the truth when I answered all his questions that only his mother would have known."

"And my soul?" When Cara did not answer him, Jericho gave a bitter laugh. "That's okay, I can guess. I bet it's not white. Am I right?"

Cara nodded her head. "It's black," she whispered.

"And I take it that's bad."

Cara nodded.

"Have you seen many black souls?" he asked.

"No."

"Why not? I don't imagine I'm the only one with a black soul."

"No, you are not, but I don't see them. They are given a different escort."

"Dare I ask?

"Grimm."

"As in the Grimm Reaper?"

Cara jumped in her seat when he started laughing.

"Excuse me, but it's really not funny." Cara's eyes darted around inside and outside the truck. "I wouldn't laugh. He really, really doesn't like being laughed at."

"What are you looking for? Could you see him if he were here?"

"I don't know. I haven't seen any other immortals since my arrival. I don't know if they are not around or if I just can't see them."

"But you could see them before, just not now. What happened?"

"I am now mortal. Someone tried to kill my sisters and I."

He gave her a hard look before activating his blinker, pulling into the gas station. Without asking her anymore questions, he pulled the truck to a stop.

"Do you have any money?" When she shook her head, he reached into his pocket and pulled out several bills and then gave them to her. "Go inside and call a cab or call someone for a ride. I'm going to grab a few groceries. Be gone when I get back." He then got out of the truck and walked away without another word.

Chapter Five

Twenty minutes later, it had begun raining as Jericho returned to his truck where there was no sign of Cara. He was extremely thankful she was out of his hair. As he was storing his groceries in the back, he double-checked to make sure she hadn't hidden once again under the tarp. Jericho refused to feel guilt at leaving her behind.

By the time he was driving away from the gas station, it had become a downpour.

It wasn't far from the turnoff to his house. At this time of year, a heavy downpour such as this could cause flash flooding and he wanted to make it home before the roads became impassable.

He hadn't gotten very far when he suddenly had to swerve to miss a figure walking in the road. Cursing, he moved the truck to the edge of the road before stopping.

"Are you trying to get yourself killed?" he yelled as he jumped out into the pouring rain. "You're walking in the middle of the fucking road!"

"I can't walk in the mud," she yelled back.

Yanking her by the arm, he dragged her to the truck, opening the door and then lifted her inside roughly before angrily slamming the door behind her.

He waited until he was once again driving before starting to yell at her again. "Why didn't you call a cab?"

"Where would I have gone? I don't know anyone or have anyplace to go."

Jericho looked at her through the dim light. There were no tears in her eyes; she was just stating a fact. What he did notice, though, was her shivering. She was freezing. "Pull off that wet coat." Flipping his heater switch, he watched for his turnoff before carefully maneuvering the truck onto the waterlogged road. It took well over an hour to reach his cabin on the dangerous road.

Even with the unwanted woman next to him, Jericho was glad to be home. The only thing that had kept him sane while sharing the cramped hotel room with his crew was the thought of being able to come home as soon as the job was done. It was why he had pushed his men so hard; the bonus money would enable him to stay home longer between jobs. It gave him the freedom of the mountains, no timetables to keep, and mainly, the ability of just being able to breathe the fresh air. The hardest thing about the memories of his prison time was the smell. The smell of unwashed bodies, urine and fear could never be forgotten.

"Get out."

Cara didn't wait for a polite invitation, she knew it wouldn't be coming. They ran to the cabin as lightning overhead provided the light to the dark porch. It only took Jericho a few seconds before he was unlocking the door and ushering her inside.

When he turned the lights on, Cara was surprised. The only furniture in the room was a plain couch and a chair placed in front of the stone fireplace.

"This way." He led her down a hallway to a darkened room. Entering, he again turned on the lights, showing a small room with a bed covered in a brown quilt and a dresser as its only contents.

Cara frowned, there was something missing from his home, though she couldn't place her finger on what was wrong.

"Here, put these on while I pack the groceries in and fix us something to eat." Thrusting a bundle of clothes in her hands that he had pulled out of the dresser, he turned and left the room, closing the door behind him. Cara quickly pulled off her drenched clothes, pulling on soft, black pants that were too long and kept sliding off her hips, and a black sweatshirt that fell to her knees and swallowed her arms, but finally returned the warmth to her body. Cara didn't know what to do with her wet clothes so she took them with her as she left to find Jericho.

She wandered through until she found him in the kitchen. As she entered, he looked up from what he was doing.

"I'm making us some sandwiches." Seeing she was holding her clothes, Jericho picked up a plate and handed it to her. "Sit down and eat." Taking her clothes, he left the room for several minutes before returning and taking the other plate. He then sat down next to her at the small table.

They ate quietly. Cara didn't know what to say, so nervously, she watched him eat.

She wasn't an expert on looks of mortal men, but even compared to the Gods, Cara knew he was outstanding. Her stomach clenched at his fierce good looks. Cara frowned at her choice of words, but it was the truth. His features were almost patrician with cold grey eyes that were emotionless. He wasn't overly tall for a man, Cara guessed he was six feet, but he was built, all muscle. The Gods loved to show off theirs with every opportunity, but even with a shirt covering his, they were very evident. Lean hipped and with a butt that looked firm beneath his faded pants, Cara would bet that if Aphrodite or Venus got a hold of him, he wouldn't be seen for decades. The Goddesses' love of good-looking men was well known, but Cara had a feeling that this was one mortal who could take care of himself. Probably even giving them a lesson or two.

Cara realized she had quit eating and that he was staring back at her, having finished his food. She turned red and, looking away, finished eating her food. The scraping of the chair told Cara that he had left the table.

Jericho put his empty plate in the sink to be washed later. He knew she had been staring at his body and despite the woman's beauty, there was no way he was going to lay a hand on that trouble. If he had been like the men he worked with, she would have already been underneath his pumping hips in his bedroom. He had no doubt that all of his men who had been separated from their women for the last six months were now making up for lost time. Nine months from now, the company would be bitching at the rise in insurance rates due to all the babies being born. If the rain hadn't stopped him, he would now have been in town showing Tammy just how many times he could get his dick up in one night.

It wasn't because of Tammy that he wasn't taking the fruitcake at his table to bed, but because there was no way he was getting involved in her mess. She was TROUBLE and he had learnt a long time ago to stay away from other people's messes. It was safer for his sanity; he would never allow himself to be locked up again. Going back to the table, he took her empty plate.

"Go to bed. In the morning, I'll drive you into town."

Cara looked at him, sensing he was in a dangerous mood. If she asked or pleaded for his help, he was more likely to throw her out in the pouring rain.

"Where will I sleep?" Cara tried to keep her voice from trembling. It suddenly seemed too much. Being made mortal, worrying about her sisters' safety and this big muscled jerk being mean to her was almost too much for her. Cara took the word back as soon as she thought it. Jericho wasn't being mean to her. He hadn't left her walking in the rain, nor wet or hungry. He was even giving a strange woman that he truly believed was crazy a bed in his home for the night.

"In the room where you changed. There's a bathroom in there also. Towels are in the bathroom closet. If you need anything, my room is across the hall." Cara nodded and left him washing dishes in the sink.

Cara entered the bedroom, wishing it was warmer. She simply couldn't get the chill out of her bones. Tiredness overwhelmed her, tempting her to just crawl under the covers and sleep. Instead, she went to the bathroom, which was as clean as the rest of his home. It took her several minutes of fiddling before she could figure out the purpose of the shower and to get the temperature of the water to warm her cold flesh.

Afterwards, she dressed in a warm shirt that she had found in Jericho's drawers, which fell to her knees like the last one. After she had pulled on the pants she had worn for dinner, she finally felt warm. Quickly, she slid into bed, pulling the warm quilt over her. Within seconds, the warmth and the sound of the storm outside comforted her to sleep.

The next morning when Cara left her room, she found Jericho talking on the phone.

"Food's in the kitchen."

Cara nodded and went into the kitchen, finding a plate of food sitting on the counter. She was almost finished when she looked up to find that Jericho was standing in the doorway watching her.

"My neighbor's basement is flooding with all the rain. I need to go over and help him. Would you like to go?"

"Yes, but what about taking me to town?"

Jericho shrugged. "The road to town is closed with the rain. It's too dangerous to try it now. When the rain stops, then I'll be able to take you." Lifting a dark brow, he asked, "Anxious to go?"

"Not at all. I just thought you were anxious to get rid

of me."

"Not at the cost of getting my truck stuck in the mud or getting killed in the flood waters. If you're done, I washed the clothes you were wearing. Get changed and we'll go."

Cara put her plate in the sink and then took the clothes that he had washed for her. It only took her a few minutes to get changed and it wasn't long before she was following Jericho outside to his truck. The lightning of the night before was gone, yet the rain was still coming down in sheets.

The road to his neighbor's house was in terrible shape. Cara had to hold on to the dashboard to keep herself in her seat and that was with the seatbelt on. She felt the truck sliding a couple of times and glanced nervously outside her window. If anyone would have told her that one day she would be terrified of heights, she would have laughed at them, but hanging off the edge of a mountain in a truck that was more off the road than on scared her silly. It was funny how mortality changed your way of thinking. Cara thanked every God she had ever met when Jericho finally pulled off the road and into the driveway of a home.

Now *this* was a home. Cara admired the beautiful log home that had been built so that it faced the breathtaking view. The porch had a swing and flowers were growing everywhere. This home showed the personality of the owners before Cara had taken a step into the interior.

Jericho introduced her to an older couple waiting in the doorway. The frail woman looked much older than the man who stood lovingly by her side, holding her hand.

"Thanks for coming, Jericho. That sump pump has gone out again and if it's not fixed soon, Mary and I will be going skinny dipping."

"Edward! He's just joking, Jericho. Go with him and I'll take care of Cara." Hesitating, Jericho gave Cara a hard look before he followed Edward out of the room.

"Would you like a cup of coffee?"

"I would love one." Cara smiled down at the tiny woman and watched as Mary slowly led her into a room. It was beautiful. The flowered couch and chairs were highlighted by a multi-colored braided rug on the wooden floor. The room was obviously an extension of this woman's unique personality.

"I had Edward fix it before you came. Jericho told him he would be bringing you."

Mary didn't ask what her relationship with Jericho was, even though Cara could see the curiosity in her tired, pain-filled eyes. Cara noticed when she went to lift the cup of coffee that her fingers trembled.

"Here let me." Cara took the cup and thanked her. "You have a beautiful home."

"Thank you. I know it's a bit flowery, but Edward puts up with it."

Cara smiled. "Have you been married for a long time?"

Mary laughed. "Thirty-six years." Her voice was proud of their accomplishment before it saddened. "We wanted to hit the forty year mark, but I don't think we're going to make it."

"I'm sorry." No, they weren't going to make it to their forty-year anniversary. Cara doubted if the woman realized just how close to death she was. She had seen the woman's soul as soon as she had walked toward her on the front porch. Her beautiful soul was fading away. "And your husband?"

"Edward is as healthy as a horse. Thank goodness he is a young man still." Mary gave Cara a wicked smile. "Even after thirty-six years of marriage he makes my heart beat faster. Hopefully he'll find someone new to share his life with. I don't want him to be alone. They say that men who've had a happy marriage tend to remarry. Do you think that is true?"

Cara looked into the woman's troubled eyes and tried to hold back her tears. Mary did not want or need her tears, she needed reassurance. "I believe so. I'm sure he will find someone when the time is right." Mary gave her a smile, changing the subject. "Have you known Jericho long?"

"No. Only a couple of days. I'm afraid I am imposing on him. The weather is keeping him from getting rid of me."

"I doubt your staying with him is much of a hardship for him." Mary looked at the beautiful young woman. For some reason her presence comforted her, as if her body ached less, and the dread and fear that was much worse than the pain ever could be, eased. She didn't feel as alone or as afraid. Mary couldn't explain it, didn't try, she merely accepted it with thankfulness.

"Jericho has lived on this mountain for ten years, and I've never known him to let a woman in his home. He hires Edward to keep it clean for him while he's away on his jobs. I was surprised he moved up here, but when the Indian council offered him the property, he accepted and built his own cabin."

"Indian council?"

Mary nodded, leaning forward to pour herself another cup of coffee. "Yes, this mountain, plus twelve thousand surrounding acres and the town are Indian owned. There are provisions that if individuals could prove their Indian heritage, then they were given a select amount of land to build their own home. Everything at one time belonged to one family, but it was turned over to the council with certain provisions, such as the one that gave the land."

"So Jericho is Native American?"

"Yes, Jericho's father was a Comanche. It was what led him to this mountain in the first place, trying to find his father."

"His father was no longer here?"

Mary sadly shook her head. "No, he had died before Jericho's birth. It's a sad story really, and the day is dreary enough, don't you think?" Cara admired the subtle way Mary changed the subject.

The women heard the men coming. "I guess they're finished."

"Can you stay for a cup of coffee, Jericho?" Mary questioned as he entered the room.

"No, thanks. We better get going before the roads get worse." Cara didn't see how much worse they could get, but stood up to leave.

She hugged a surprised Mary goodbye. "It was an honor to meet you." Jericho waited impatiently for her to say her goodbyes, but Cara wasn't going to be rushed. As she passed Edward, she took his hand. "It was also nice to meet you."

"It was nice to meet you also. Please come back and visit. Mary could use the company."

"I would like that." Cara meant to leave without another word, she really did. After all, she had been trained since birth not to interfere. The consequences were always known, and Cara and her sisters had never once disobeyed. However those consequences no longer applied. She had already lost her powers, she was mortal. Surely, just this once, the rules could be bent, if not broken.

Cara tightened her hand around Edward's and lowered her voice so Mary, who was gathering the dishes, could not hear. "You must not do what you are planning."

Startled, Edward tried to pull his hand from her grasp. "I don't know what you're talking about."

"Yes you do, and it will not work. You will be separated, never to find each other again. Be patient and she will be returned to you."

"I can't lose her." His tormented words tore at Cara's heart.

"You won't if you wait, but if you go through with your plans, you will lose her forever."

Jericho jerked her arm, forcing her to release Edward's hand. "I apologize, Edward. I shouldn't have brought her." Jericho turned, dragging her from the house.

"Stop it; I'm coming." Cara tried to get her arm away,

but was successful only when Jericho had her in the truck once again, slamming the door.

"How could you do that to that old couple? It was downright cruel, and what were you telling him not to do anyway?"

"He plans to kill himself when Mary dies. He can't bear the thought of a life without her."

"And you know this how? Did Mary say something?"

"No, she doesn't know. He knows it would break her heart. And I am able to see the color of his soul matches Mary's; it is already preparing to leave. Edward's should not have been that way, Mary said he was healthy."

Jericho reversed carefully until they were once again on the dangerous road. He needed his head examined for even taking Cara around his neighbors, especially as sick as Mary was.

Jericho frowned; Edward had seemed to know what Cara was talking about. Jericho had thought that Edward was dealing with Mary's upcoming death well; his planned suicide would explain his unexpected acceptance of losing a wife of so many years. How had Cara known? Had Mary secretly hinted it to Cara or had the girl just guessed. One thing was for sure, the sooner he got rid of her, the better. When was this damn rain ever going to stop?

Chapter Six

Odin's court was filled to capacity. Fate stood in the back of the huge hall and watched as the beautiful Goddesses vied for his attention. Their filmy gowns left nothing to the imagination, each hoping to be the one he chose for an evening of pleasure.

Fate's lip curled in disgust when Venus sat in his lap to hold a goblet to his lips. When a small amount of wine clung to his lips, she slid forward, her tongue licking his lips before giving him a voracious kiss. Fate heard her moans in the back of the crowed hall. The stupid slut's butt ground harder against Odin's lap, trying to bring herself to an orgasm.

If the task she was there for was not so important, Fate would have left then. Instead, she slowly moved forward to Odin's dais. As the other's realized she was there, they moved back, allowing an unobstructed path. Fate didn't wonder at their movements, so accustomed to it. They feared her; afraid she would somehow know their thoughts, actions and feelings. They were right.

Odin watched the woman walk toward him, knew the smile playing on her lips was because she believed everyone feared her. She was wrong. The women were jealous of her beauty and moved away because they didn't want her to know, and the men skittered away in embarrassment at their body's arousal. Fate was a stunningly beautiful woman with a body that was every man or God's idea of perfection.

The only thing that saved her from the Goddesses' jealousy was her power. None dared to harm the woman. She had gifts and powers unlike any other. If that wasn't enough, she held the friendship of the couple literally holding the powers of the universe in their hands.

Fate was afraid of no one and feared by all. All except Odin. Of course it helped that Chronas was his father, so therefore, he did not fear retribution as other immortals.

His eyes narrowed as she stopped before him. Her Grecian gown was made of silk and clung to every luscious curve and line on her body. When the arrogant beauty kneeled before him, providing a glimpse of her firm breasts as her head bowed, it took every ounce of control he possessed to keep from grabbing her and taking her on the floor. Only his pride saved him from making an ass of himself and kept his expression an unreadable mask.

"Fate, why am I granted the pleasure of seeing you on your knees before me?"

His sarcasm made Fate want to throw the wine goblet at his head. Instead, she lowered her voice, seductive and full of promises she had no intention of fulfilling. "I beg a favor, your highness."

Odin laughed at her submissive tone. This woman didn't have a submissive bone in her body. His body had taken several days to recover from the night he had spent in her bed.

"I wait breathlessly to see just what this favor entails to bring you to your knees. Dare I guess it involves the disappearance of your daughters?"

"May we speak privately?"

"Rise, Fate. As much as I enjoy you on your knees

before me, this fake meekness grows tiresome." As she rose gracefully to her feet, he lifted a hand. "Leave us."

Venus reluctantly slid off his lap, giving Fate a dirty look. Fate ignored the stupid bitch; she had other more pressing matters than who was next in line for a romp with Odin. She could have him and her look told her so.

Odin's hand tightened on the arms of his throne, barely restraining himself from crushing it in his anger. He had seen the look she had given Venus and knew she felt nothing other than contempt for the women begging for his favor. He wanted to throttle the woman, right after he fucked her senseless.

When the court was empty, Odin's voice boomed out in the hollow room, "What is it you want, Fate?"

"Get Thor to grant me an audience." Odin knew that was why she had come. It had been her only recourse to regaining her daughters. Fate could not enter Thor's palace without permission; it remained the one and only place that she could not appear without direct invitation.

"You're going to ask him for help?" Odin leaned back on his throne. "I'm curious, Fate, why you are not asking for my help? I could retrieve them for you, why not beg me?"

"I would not ask you to break your oath to Mother." Odin had given an oath to Mother never to interfere on Earth again, since the last time he had taken hundreds of lives in anger.

Odin nodded. "And what favor would you grant me for asking my son to listen to you? You know I cannot make him aide you, only to listen to your request."

"I hope I can convince him to help me." Fate shrugged. "But I can't ask for his help unless he sees me. That is why I need your help. Whatever you want in payment, I will pay."

"Anything, Fate? Be careful if you do not mean your words. Once we strike a bargain, I will not allow you to renege on it because you have achieved your goals."

Fate stiffened. "I give you my word, and once given, I will stand by it until our bargain is met. What do you want in return for an audience with Thor?"

"You in my bed for as long as I wish," Odin spoke carefully. When setting a trap, the hunter must never let his prey know their ultimate goal. He knew what her answer would be before she spoke.

"One night," Fate countered.

Odin shrugged nonchalantly. "It was worth a try. Very well, Fate; one night, but be warned, this time I won't play the part of Valentine so that you can pretend to yourself that you don't want me. This time, you will know it's me from beginning to end."

"Agreed, but I have one stipulation."

"And that is?"

"I will not see the bargain met until all three of my daughters are safely home." Odin admired her. She was a hell of an adversary. She planned to outsmart him; she had no intention of seeing their bargain met. As always, though, Fate underestimated him. He was about to prove her wrong.

"Very well. We're agreed. I'll send for Thor."

Fate breathed a sigh of relief. "Thank you, Odin." Turning, she started to leave in a hurry to once again check on her daughters' movements. However Odin stopped her before she could leave.

"What makes you think he will help you? He hates you, Fate." Fate turned back to the obnoxious God.

"I know this, but as much as he hates me as his mother, he loves his sisters."

* * *

Jericho did not speak once they were back at the cabin, showing his anger in silence. Not that he talked to her more than he had to before, yet now he simply disappeared into his room, leaving her by herself. Cara sat on the couch and watched the rain outside the window.

She sighed, not much had changed from her home.

Her sisters and mother often left her by herself. Cara had become used to being lonely. She got up and wandered aimlessly around the small room. The lack of color and homey feel was in direct contrast to Mary's home. There were no photos or personal possessions of any kind sitting around. Not even a comfortable rug just lying around on the wood floors. It was as stark and cold as the man himself.

Cara frowned. She had spoken the truth when she had told him that his soul was black. There was something she had not told him that she had never seen before; a slight shade of gold had flickered within the darkness. Gold souls were the mark of immortals. His was very slight, as to be almost nonexistent. In fact, she would have missed seeing it if not for the amount of time she spent staring at the man. He pretended not to notice her staring, and as much as she tried, Cara couldn't help herself. She wanted to touch his hard face and see gentleness, see desire in his eyes, which always were void of any emotion.

The Gods and Goddess were well known for their sexual exploits, yet Fate had kept Cara and her sisters away from the excesses. Cara had never been tempted even by the most handsome of the Gods, yet Jericho made her want him with no encouragement. This was hard for a woman to admit when her father was a Saint.

"Are you hungry?" Cara jumped when Jericho spoke from the kitchen. She hadn't even heard him walk through the room. Blushing, Cara nodded her head.

Jericho gave her a hard look. "Is spaghetti, okay?"

"I've never had it before, but I've been enjoying trying new things." Cara walked to the kitchen and watched as he cooked. It was very interesting watching him work around the kitchen because he was unselfconscious about his movements.

She watched as he put long strands of something into a steaming pot while the smell coming from the pan of red sauce he had been working on was appetizing. Her stomach growled. Cara put a hand to her rumbling stomach and laughed.

"You should have told me you were so hungry." He reached toward the counter and pulled a large piece of bread off the loaf sitting there.

"I did not realize that I was. Everything smells so good." Cara watched as Jericho moved the sauce to the counter. Thinking to help him, she reached and touched the steaming pot, wanting to move it to the counter. Searing pain in her hands was instantaneous.

"What the hell have you done?" Deftly, he moved the pot away from the stove to the counter and quickly grabbed her hands pulling her towards the sink before turning on the water to run it over her red palms. The cold water soothed the pain, but not for long.

"Dammit, why did you touch it without a towel?"

"I didn't know," Cara's voice trembled. It was everything she could do not to howl in pain. Tears filled her eyes. When she was immortal, she would have been unable to hurt herself. She had to learn caution now that her body had become mortal.

"Haven't you cooked food before?"

"No, my mother's servants prepare our meals."

"Must be nice." Cara could tell by his look of disgust that he was being sarcastic. Her shoulders drooped. Now he thought that not only was she crazy, but helpless as well.

"Stay still, I'll be right back."

Within minutes, he was back. Turning off the water, he dried her hands with a clean towel. Afterwards, he rubbed a soothing lotion on her burning hands. He was gentle and careful not to hurt her stinging hands. When he was done, he wrapped them in gauze.

"Take these," he instructed, holding two tablets in his hands. Cara looked at them quizzically. "Just aspirin for the pain. I'm sorry, I don't have anything stronger." Cara took them with the glass of water he handed her.

"Now sit down while I see if I can save our dinner." Cara sat at the table, feeling useless as she watched him fix their plates.

It took only a few minutes before he slid the plate of pasta in front of her. Cara could only think of one thing as she dug into her plate of food. Heaven, pure Heaven. It was the most delicious dish she had ever tasted. At first, she had trouble eating the stringy mess, but after watching Jericho twirl it onto his fork, she followed suit. The taste was exquisite. She cleaned her plate using a chunk of bread to sop up the remains of the tangy sauce, imitating Jericho.

"Would you like some more?" For the first time, Cara actually saw a small smile on his face. Cara was struck dumb. She took it back; if Venus or Aphrodite saw him, they would never let him leave their bed. For the first time, Cara wished she had watched their maneuvering with the opposite sex. Maybe then she wouldn't be feeling so inept at how to act.

At his questioning look, Cara realized he was still waiting for her answer. "Yes, please."

While he was fixing her another plate, Cara reached out and carefully refilled her wine glass.

"I'd be careful if I were you. You had a shock to your system with the burns then the aspirin. It might not be wise to drink too much wine."

Cara waved his concern away with a bandaged hand. "I'll be fine. We have wine with our meals at home, and ours is much stronger than yours."

"If you say so." They both dug into their food and it wasn't long before they sat back stuffed.

"I may never move again. That was the best meal I've ever had. Thank you."

"You're welcome. It was just spaghetti, though."

"It was ambrosia." Jericho looked at the beautiful woman, who was barely able to remain sitting upright. She was on her third glass of wine.

Jericho frowned. The last thing he wanted to deal with

was an intoxicated woman who had mental challenges while he had been without a good fuck for six months. He ignored her natural sexiness when her little, pink tongue licked a small drop of sauce from a wine glazed lip.

"You better get to bed while the wine has eased the pain in your hands." He started clearing the table as she got up.

"Goodnight."

"Goodnight."

Jericho breathed a sigh of relief, glad the temptation of a woman was out of his sight. He had no intention of getting involved with the woman. The only use he had for a woman was on her back with her legs wrapped firmly around his waist, and Cara was trouble, pure temptation; Jericho knew better than to tempt fate.

Chapter Seven

Cara woke early the next morning with the bright sunshine pouring through the window. She dressed slowly, knowing Jericho would drive her into town as soon as possible. She walked slowly into the living room, and she wasn't wrong. He was waiting for her with his keys in hand.

"I'll get my coat."

Jericho refused to feel guilty at the hurt look in her eyes.

When she returned wearing her coat, they walked to the truck where he silently opened the door for her, mindful of her hurt hands.

The ride into town was silent. Haden was a small town with a small population, yet the main road was backed up with traffic.

"I wonder what's going on. I've never seen the town this busy." Jericho saw several of the cars had out of town license plates as he parked his truck in front of the diner.

"Let's grab a bite to eat and then I'll help you find a place to stay." Cara followed him into a small diner.

They sat at a booth that a small family left as they

entered. As the family passed by, Cara winked at the small child held in her mother's arms. Not long after Jericho had handed her a menu, wanting the ordeal over, she looked up when a perky brunette came to their table with a pad in her hand. Her brightly colored lips curled into a smile that Cara had seen on Venus and Aphrodite's lips hundreds of times. Cara looked at Jericho to see his reaction, which was an answering smile.

Cara's heart ached; she had wanted him to look at her that way, not another woman. The only consolation she had was the smile never reached his eyes, they stayed just as hard and cold. He might desire the woman, however she didn't have his heart. Cara was beginning to realize no woman would be able to claim that part of him. It did not exist.

"When did you get back into town?" As her hand reached out to run down his muscled arm, Cara wanted to reach out and smack the woman's hand away from him.

"Couple of days ago. We've been rained in at the cabin. Tammy, this is Cara," Jericho introduced them without looking up from his menu. He showed that neither woman was of importance to him.

Cara's lips tightened. She wanted to throw the glass of water in his face, yet barely restrained her temper. She was the most even-tempered of her sisters. Often they had made fun of her attitude, not understanding how she could be so forgiving of others, but Jericho was pushing at her anger.

She could understand his attitude towards her. She had been thrust upon him and he had seen that she had been taken care of, but this Tammy had obviously shared his bed and he could have at least been courteous. Cara could tell the woman was trying to keep the anger and jealously hidden from Jericho when a fake smile curved her lips.

"She's looking for a place to stay. After we eat, we'll head to the hotel and then I'll wait until you get off."

The other woman's eyes brightened. "The inn is

booked solid. There was a massive mudslide and the highway is closed until they can get it cleared. The town is full of stranded motorists. But I have an idea; she could stay at my place. Hopefully, I won't need it for a few days."

Jericho raised his eyes from the menu. He had never allowed her to stay at his cabin, but it was the lesser of two evils. He needed to get rid of Cara before he made a mistake he would regret. Tammy knew the score; she would never expect more from him than a quick fuck. Cara, on the other hand, would expect more, and Jericho had no intention of giving her false hope. He wanted no woman permanently. He didn't want a woman other than relieving his needs, and once the sex was over, he wanted her gone. It would be a pain having Tammy in his cabin, but the road would open soon and he could bring her back and put Cara in the inn.

"That sounds like a plan," Jericho told Tammy.

"Great. I get off at five. What can I get you to eat?"

Jericho ordered his steak and looked at Cara. "What would you like to eat?" He hardened himself against her hurt filled gaze.

"Do they have spaghetti?" This time it was Jericho who looked away. He felt as if he had kicked a helpless kitten. Forcing indifference, he looked at Tammy. "Give her the same thing I ordered."

When Tammy left to get their orders of food, Cara looked down. She didn't know what to do. She didn't want to be left alone in town while Jericho took his waitress back to the cabin. She knew they would spend the time in his bed, which made her so envious of the woman she couldn't breathe. If Venus or Aphrodite were here, they would know how to get their man, however Cara had no idea of what to do.

When the door to the restaurant opened, Cara looked to see who was entering. Her breath caught in her throat. She didn't think she would ever be glad to see the man who entered, yet right now, when she was missing her family so badly and suffering from Jericho's rejection, she was so happy that tears came into her eyes.

The other diners weren't so happy. The women were stunned at his sensual beauty and every hormone went into overdrive. Their bodies squirmed in desire, breasts tautened, eyes glazed over as they watched the man poised in the doorway. Grimm always liked to make an entrance.

As Cara's face lit up and an angelic smile curved her luscious lips, Jericho's dick hardened in his jeans. He forced himself to look away from her; to stare out the window and gain control of himself. The sooner he got Tammy back to his cabin, the better. She was uncomplicated and would take care of the hard on he'd had since meeting Cara.

Cara watched in amusement as Grimm's dark eyes searched the faces of the diners. The men choked on fear while every misdeed, whether minor or truly evil, flashed before their eyes. Every primitive instinct of both sexes had been brought to the forefront. Guilty husbands looked away from their wives, the women shied away from their husbands in remorse, even the children were affected, beginning to cry and confess to every misdeed; from disobeying the babysitter to swiping candy at the local market.

When he began to walk toward Cara's table, the people in the restaurant actually tensed in fear that he would stop at their own.

Jericho, oblivious to the man entering the room, only turned from staring out the window when the man slid in next to him at the booth they were sitting at.

Surprise stilled him from knocking the intruder away.

"Hello, sweetheart."

Tears clogged her throat and she was barely able to squeak out his name. "Grimm"

"How are you holding up?"

Cara gathered herself. "It's good to see you. Have you

come to take me home?" Hope lit her beautiful eyes.

"Sorry, babe, you know that's not possible. I was in the neighborhood and thought I would stop in to see how you're doing." Cara's lip began to tremble before she could help herself.

"I want to go home. Please help me, Grimm." Desperation was in her voice.

She had to get away from Jericho. Cara felt in her mortal bones how badly he could hurt her; what he had just done was merely a small taste of it. He had rejected her for another woman. Her pride stung and she simply wanted to go home to her mother. Her mother would protect her and make sure no overbearing man would dare treat her daughter in such a manner.

"I would if I could, but you know I can't. It's not your time. Besides, you know that if I took you, it wouldn't be home that I would have to take you to."

Cara nodded. Suddenly fear filled her gorgeous face. "You're not here to…?" She glanced in fear at Jericho. An evil smiled curled Grimm's lips at her look.

"Nope, not him either. I'm on a layover you might say. I have a little time and thought I would find something to amuse myself with." Cara felt sorry for this amusement. Grimm would be like a tiger amusing itself with a small mouse. Tormenting it to death. Death and Grimm were always a foregone conclusion.

Jericho sat stiffly next to the man who Cara had called Grimm. He wanted answers, and this man looked like anything other than a loony. Perhaps Cara wasn't mentally ill, but part of a scam with this stranger. As if the man could read his thoughts, he turned to give Jericho his full attention.

"My little friend has been remiss in her introductions. Allow me. I am Grimm and you are Jericho Hawk." When Jericho stared into the man's black eyes, he felt as if his soul literally shrunk back inside himself. Hiding. Jericho tried to shrug the analogy away, yet was unable to stop himself. The man put out a coldness that actually made you shiver. Jericho didn't look away. He had faced and survived worse monsters than this man. The problem was, Jericho inexplicably was beginning to believe that this Grimm was no ordinary man. It was hard to miss the reactions of the other patrons when everyone was staring at your table. "I hope you have been taking good care of her." Threats glittered in the dark gaze staring at him.

Grimm's eyes looked at Cara's bandaged hands and darkened further.

Cara jumped in quickly. "It was my fault; I wasn't careful."

"You must be more careful, Cara. If anything happened to you, my anger would not be pleasant." Grimm turned once again to Jericho, making sure the other man got his message.

Jericho had had enough of the man's threats. "I'm glad you're here." Smirking to himself at Grimm's surprised look. Jericho was sure it didn't happen often. "You can take Cara off my hands and see that she is taken care of. After all, you two are obviously close." Innuendo heavily laced his voice, leaving no doubt at what he thought their true relationship was. Jericho really didn't care who they were fucking, though.

He'd had enough. He tried to push the man so that he could slide out of the booth and leave the two alone while he waited for Tammy in his truck until she got off work. Suddenly, he fell back in his seat and Grimm hadn't even moved. Fury emitted from the man's expression. Jericho no longer felt the coldness the man put out; instead, red-hot heat surged through his body.

"Grimm!" Jericho dimly heard Cara's scream, but he was unable to look away from the deadly black eyes.

Visions exploded within his skull. Cara standing on a balcony, staring into a dark sky. He felt the loneliness and sadness she felt. Then other visions flew through his mind. Her standing in a corner watching a party of individuals.

Many of the women were dressed in flowing gowns and the men dressed as warriors. Instantly, Jericho knew who each person was as if he had known them for years, and realized he was reading Cara's mind at the moment of the party. Envy of the other women's obvious sexuality, and painfully shy when an immortal dared to talk to her under her mother's watchful glare.

Cara hid a deep-rooted fear that she would never be able to match the greatness of her mother and aunt. Then everything in his mind dimmed as if he was in a dark tunnel. He heard women's screams of terror and choking fear for her sisters' safety. Flashes of light allowed Jericho to see Cara struggle to watch the doorways her sisters went through before she allowed herself to find an exit, putting her own life at risk.

Jericho was stunned when he felt the seat once again beneath him. He didn't know how the man had done it, but he knew that he could no longer argue against Cara's story; he had seen it all. She was what she had said. Someone had tried to kill her and they had almost succeeded. Now she was left stripped of her powers.

"What did you do?" Cara questioned anxiously, well aware of Grimm's powers.

"Took away his doubts. He now knows that you speak the truth."

"You shouldn't have done that. You could be punished."

Grimm shrugged. "Who would dare punish me?" Cara knew he was right. He could take a mortal or immortal soul with a touch. It was a power he exerted with effortless ease.

"Why?"

"I owed you one." Cara understood what he was saying. Often they had argued over souls. She had felt circumstances should have been taken into account when determining a soul's destination. Grimm had not; he had only been interested in the end result. Cara had believed that a single transgression regretted and mourned over shouldn't lead to Grimm, yet he more often than not had won and she had lost numerous souls to him.

"If you're done, now will you two please leave?"

Grimm didn't take his attention away from Cara. "He's really making me angry, sweetheart."

"Jericho." Cara thought to warn him, but it was too late.

Grimm moved with lightning speed, grabbing Jericho's wrist and holding it in a brutal grip he was unable to break in the small confines of the booth. In the same instant, he took Cara's hand.

Memories flooded her mind. Jericho as a small child neglected and left alone by an uncaring mother, foster homes until he had ended up with a woman he had thought of as a monster, but she was more than that. She had been one of such malicious evil that Cara, for all her centuries of seeing souls, had rarely seen. She had been given the care of a small child who had never known love or affection, and had tried to destroy what humanity he had left. He had been both mentally and physically abused to such an extent that Cara tried to shake her hand free from Grimm's grip, unable to bear seeing the torture he had been forced to endure for years.

Grimm refused to relinquish her hand, forcing her to see and feel everything that Jericho had borne for years at the evil woman's hands. When he was finally old enough to escape the woman, she had been unable to handle not having her toy to torture and had tried to regain her power over him. It had led to her death by his hands. He had even been imprisoned for the murder until it had finally been proved to be self-defense. Cara saw the years he spent alone, knowing his soul had been scarred beyond repair.

Cara swallowed back the tears. A child learnt love from his caretakers and then would be able to share that love with others. Jericho had never learnt to love. Everyone had failed the child, and the man had paid the price.

Grimm released their hands.

"What did you do?" Jericho angrily questioned him.

"Merely gave Cara a heads-up."

"What does that mean?"

"It means that you shouldn't make me angry." He turned and gave Jericho a smile of intent just as Tammy came to the table with their order. The poor woman couldn't stop shaking as she placed their plates before them.

"Can I get you something?" The woman's tone suggested he could have anything he wanted.

"Well, now, what are you offering, sweetness?" Seduction poured from Grimm's voice.

Tammy didn't beat around the bush. "Me."

Cara thought the woman would rip her clothes off then and there. If her nipples got any larger, they were going to burst through her uniform.

Grimm smiled seductively at the lust-crazed woman. "Well, I could use a place to stay since I'm trapped here with the roads closed."

"I have a place close by, you could stay with me." Grimm smiled even wider, showing his pearly whites. "I was supposed to meet Jericho, but I would rather have you," Tammy confessed guiltily.

"What time do you get off?" Grimm's predatory smile widened.

"Give me a minute, I'll be right back." She turned away, but then hesitated, turning back to Grimm. "I will have to make up an excuse to my boss." At his nod of approval, Tammy rushed off.

"That was bad, Grimm."

"That's one of the perks of my job," he said unrepentant then gave Jericho his attention once more. "My little friend will be returning home with you, and I expect you to take better care of her than you have been." He reached out and touched each of Cara's hands, which were lying on the table, with a brief touch. Instantly, she felt the soreness leaving.

"Thanks." Cara was thanking him for more than healing her hands. She was thanking him for letting her get to know Jericho in ways it would have taken years for a mortal to know, if ever, because Jericho would never have told. Most of all, she was thanking him for getting the horny waitress away from Jericho.

"Happy to oblige." Grimm slid out of the booth when Tammy returned. When she leaned into his body, he placed an arm around her hip to draw her against his side while smiling wickedly.

"I stole twenty dollars from the cash register last week," Tammy confessed suddenly.

"Did you? Then you must replace it your next payday, shouldn't you?" Grimm caressed her hip, staring deep into her eyes.

"Yes, that's a good idea. I will replace it when I get paid." Tammy closed dazed eyes when Grimm pulled her even closer in approval.

Jericho thought Tammy would climax from the gesture, disgusted with the turn of events. He didn't care about losing Tammy for the sex, what he did care about was getting rid of Cara.

"Now that I know she has relatives to take care of her, why should I take her back to my cabin? You can collect her when you've finished with her." He gave a curt nod in Tammy's direction.

"Well, that may take some time, and we don't want Cara sitting here all alone, do we? After all, the enemies who are responsible for her vacation are looking for her."

Cara stiffened, afraid not for herself, but for her sisters. If their unknown enemy was looking for her, it only made sense they would be searching for her sisters also.

"Besides, I would hate to make a phone call back to the Sheriff in Hardin to let him know that you've been with the woman he's been searching for. I don't know how these things work, but he might put you in jail for interfering with police business."

Jericho knew when he was beat. He was stuck with her until the road opened and he could get her a room at the inn. How long could it take? A day at the most. Jericho was man enough to admit when he was outmaneuvered. However he simply couldn't let Grimm leave without one final shot.

"When we meet again, I won't be stuffed into a booth, unable to move," Jericho threatened the last man he would ever want to make angry. Cara cast Grimm an imploring look not to hurt him.

Grimm turned back with the woman who was now whimpering with desire in his arms. He stroked her cheek. "Just a few more minutes, kitten." He turned his black eyes to Jericho. "The next time we meet, I won't be there to protect Cara; it will be because I'm doing my job." He hesitated long enough until he knew Jericho understood his deadly message. When Jericho met Grimm again, it would be because he would be there for his soul. Grimm couldn't resist a taunting grin before he led the now panting waitress out of the restaurant.

Jericho turned backed to his now cold food. "Eat. I know you're hungry." Cara didn't say anything, afraid he would leave her behind. He was furious with Grimm and Cara couldn't blame him. In all fairness, he had seen that she was taken care of and she had repaid him by letting Grimm treat him abominably. He had broken into the privacy of his past, taken his woman and had threatened him in a roundabout way with Hell.

"I'll get him. He can help me find a place to stay." Cara started to rise from the booth and go after Grimm. She only hoped she could catch him before he got busy with Tammy.

"Sit down." His harsh voice stopped her and she sat back down. "Eat." Then his voice softened. "When you're finished, we'll head home."

Cara nodded and dropped her head, shoving a forkful of food past the lump in her throat when he had said they would go home. Cara knew he hadn't meant it the way she had taken it to mean, however she felt the warmth spread to her now human heart.

Chapter Eight

The ride back to the cabin didn't take long. When they entered the cabin, Cara expected Jericho to leave her to her own devices, but she was pleasantly surprised.

"Would you like to watch some television?"

"Yes, thank you." They settled on the couch and Jericho used a small remote to change the machine on the wall. Cara was fascinated as the glass-front machine changed pictures.

"What kind of shows do you like?"

"I don't know."

Jericho laughed at her. "I guess you don't have television where you're from."

"No, we don't."

"Then you're in for a real treat." The pictures changed several more times before it stopped. Cara watched as two women talked then started eating something really fast.

"This is called reality television. Real people do things and people watch them at home." They watched for several minutes until the program went off then Jericho turned the pictures again until another show appeared. "This is called a comedy." It didn't take long before her soft laughter filled the small cabin.

"Would you like a beer?"

"Yes." Her throat did feel dry.

Jericho got up from the couch while Cara kept her eyes on the screen, trying not to notice how his faded jeans emphasized his well-shaped ass.

"Here you are; ice cold."

"Thank you." Cara took a small drink from the cold bottle. She knew she had discovered her second favorite thing about being human. It tasted slightly like ale, but a much weaker version. She could never stand the taste of the strong brew, but this was like a paler version and the coldness only accented its wonderful taste.

"Pretzel?" Cara took one of what looked like sticks, though it tasted crunchy and salty.

"I think I'm going to enjoy a few things about being human."

Jericho laughed at her obvious enjoyment of the snacks. She even imitated him by putting her feet up on the small table before them, sinking back in a comfortable position on the old couch. He slid closer to her on the couch, letting his thigh brush against her softer one.

"What would you be doing if you were at home?"

"I would be riding or working. I often rode when I was bored, or watched the sky. My sisters each had their own pursuits. Zerina attends births, she loved walking; she would disappear several times only to come back with tales of lands she would go exploring. Broni loves to fight. She would watch past battles and replay them over and over again. She spends a lot of time exercising her body into exhaustion."

"You had no interests to keep you occupied?"

"No, not really." A small blush colored her cheeks.

"What?"

"I would often watch and play with the servants' children."

Jericho had seen the images of her playing with the

children when Grimm had touched him. She had been running in a green field with the children chasing behind her. She had looked beautiful, from the few seconds he could remember, with her long, black hair flying around her face and her laughter filling his mind.

"I love children." A soft look entered her eyes as wishful dreams swirled within.

Jericho had seen that look before on other women's faces, so he did the only thing any normal, single, red-blooded male would do. He changed the subject by flipping the television channel until he found what he was looking for to distract her. A blood-chilling scream filled the room as a monster chased a man across the screen.

EWW! Cara was enthralled. She didn't take her eyes off the television as the horror movie became even more gruesome. Jericho was surprised she didn't cringe away and shudder at the massacre taking place. Instead, she was absorbed and started yelling suggestions at hiding places for the hapless victims. Jericho could not help laughing at her antics.

"Would you like another beer?" She nodded without taking her eyes off the movie. When he was in the kitchen, he put a pizza in the oven for later.

They sat for several hours, silently watching television and eating pizza. Cara was enjoying herself and so was Jericho.

"What are you smiling about?" Cara looked at him, seeing the smile. It was the first genuine one she had seen on his stern face.

"Nothing really, I was just thinking that this is a typical date for mortals then I realized it was a first for me also."

"You never sat and had a movie date before?"

"No, I had other things on my mind," Jericho confessed wryly.

"Such as?"

Jericho simply lifted a brow at her question.

"And you are not interested in me that way?"

"I definitely wouldn't say that." Jericho reached out and touched her creamy cheek, thinking that it could not possibly be as soft as it looked. He was wrong; it was like touching a piece of Heaven.

He knew this was a terrible idea, tried to draw back, but it was as if an irresistible force drew him towards her. He had never felt this way before and that in itself made his stomach clench in fear.

Determined, he forced himself away from her. He would have succeeded if he hadn't looked into her eyes. She wanted him. He knew what that look meant and it had been a long time since he had a woman underneath him. He swore to himself that she wouldn't be any different than any other woman he had taken to his bed. As long as she played by his rules, there was no reason they could not have an enjoyable time together. His reasoning took away the last of his restraint.

Cara sat still as Jericho slowly reached out and traced her lips with a gentle finger. His touch made her stomach clench with a feeling she had never felt before. When his lips replaced his finger, she enjoyed the feel of his firm lips against hers. She was surprised at the gentleness he showed as he pulled her closer into his body at the same time as his tongue parted her lips and showed her what a real kiss was; compared to ones she had only been able to imagine.

Her mother had been overly strict, and with a Saint for a father, she had been given no opportunity to have a sexual relationship.

Jericho took control; it was as if he knew her inexperience and took his time building her desire. He was patient.

When Jericho felt her body soften, and she began to timidly return his kisses, he let his lips trail down to her neck. He showed her how her body could shake in need when he reached her breasts. She hadn't even felt him opening the buttons until he pulled the cups of her bra down and took her nipple into his mouth. There was not a hesitant bone in Jericho's body.

Cara let out a small scream at the unbelievable pleasure. She felt herself getting wet between her thighs. She clenched them together, trying to regain her shattering control.

Jericho's hand slid down her taut stomach and when he reached out to unbutton her blue jeans. Cara reached out to stop him, shy that he would find how wet she was for him. His lips left her nipple to return to her mouth, his tongue thrusting deep at the same time his hand slid inside her jeans, finding the wetness she had tried to control.

Her embarrassment slid away as his fingers began moving within her folds of silky flesh, coaxing her to move urgently against his hand. The heat building within her flew out of control. Cara felt her breath catch and her body tightened in a spasm that relieved the pressure he had built carefully within her inexperienced body.

"What happened?" she whispered in utter bliss.

"You came."

"Oh. Is there more?"

"Yes, if you want me to."

"Show me."

"Are you sure?"

Cara nodded her head eagerly.

He removed her clothes, and when she was naked, he pushed her back until she was lying on the couch. His lips once again covered her nipple and his hand slid up her thigh, moving it until she was spread open to him. His lips traveled down her stomach, slowing as he placed gentle kisses on his path downwards.

When he nuzzled the curling hair between her thighs, she attempted to twist away, but his hands tightened on her small waist, holding her still as he found her wetness. His tongue discovered every slick fold and hidden crevice, making her burn even hotter, while her hands gripped the material of the couch to prevent herself from burying her hands in his hair to pull him closer. Jericho pulled and tugged at her with his tongue, creating suction with his lips that had her butt lifting off the couch, grinding herself against his tormenting mouth.

When his finger slid inside her, her inner muscles clenched, forcing him to withdraw and lubricate his fingers with her slippery moisture before once again sliding inside of her, easing through the tight sheath purposefully. With every twitch of her hips, his finger slid deeper until he withdrew it once again only to replace it with two fingers. When he was able to easily slide his fingers within her, he sat back on the couch. The cold air-cooled her heated flesh, bringing a moment of clear-headedness.

"Are you sure you want to do this?" He was making sure she knew what she was doing. She had drunk several beers and her first orgasm had swept her away. He wanted no recriminations thrown his way later.

Cara looked at Jericho. She knew he was giving her a chance to change her mind, yet Cara knew she wasn't going to. The color of his soul seemed to mock her decision, but she wanted him. Her body even now craved for his touch to return.

"Yes." Her voice was firm.

"Then come here." Jericho stood.

Cara thought he would take her into his bedroom. Instead, he unsnapped his jeans and removed them. Next, he pulled his shirt over his head before sitting back down on the couch then he pulled her until she was sitting astride him. He leaned forward and gave her his mouth. She loved his kisses; they made her hot and achy.

She rubbed her bare breasts against his chest as Jericho gripped her hips and lifted her slightly until his penis nestled at her wet entrance. Slowly, he pulled her down onto him, entering her inch by inch. Cara winced as the tight tissues fought his strokes.

Jericho's lips left hers to take a nipple in his mouth. Gently, he suckled and nibbled until Cara felt a rush of liquid flowing from her cunt, allowing him to push the head of his cock passed her tight entrance. He held Cara above him with hard hands that controlled each tiny movement of his cock.

When he felt her hymen, he wasn't surprised. Grimm had shown him flashes of Cara's life and a lover had not been among them. He moved to her other breast, making her squirm harder against him. When he broke through her hymen she moaned in pain, but he gave her a moment to adjust before he removed his hands and let her weight force her down on his massive length.

Cara moaned in pain again, quickly using her knees to catch the brunt of her weight. She pulled herself up until only a few inches off his hard length remained inside her tight depths.

His hand cupped her cunt, his thumb working her until moisture gushed and her muscles relaxed around his cock. Jericho crooned to her in a soft voice, easing her anxiety as he sat completely still, letting Cara set her own pace.

Afraid that the pain would return, Cara began to move up and down his cock, at first going slow and awkward, however within minutes, her knees gripped his hips and she moved faster and faster. She never allowed him to enter her more than halfway, catching her weight before she took him full length. Jericho didn't mind, he was inside her and he was about to come. It would have been cock heaven if she could have taken his size, but she was still giving him pleasure. Even women who had been sexually active had trouble with his size, so he had known Cara would be unable to take his dick without too much pain.

Cara felt as if she was once again in the clouds as she moved faster and faster above him, sliding up and down his slick length. Her cunt burned at the sensation of having something so huge shoved inside the tight confines. The feelings grew until she could no longer hold onto her response. She barely caught herself from letting her weight fall down on his penis and only the pain of his first entrance gave her enough control to hold her body above his as another, harder orgasm shook her body. As she rode the orgasm, she felt Jericho spasm inside of her and knew he had also come. With a groan, her head fell forward and lay on his chest.

Jericho allowed her a few seconds to catch her breath before gripping her hips and lifting her off him to lie on the couch next to him. She was still shuddering as he casually bent over her and brushed her breast with a steady hand. A satisfied smile curved his lips when her nipple hardened and her hips lifted toward him.

"Are you okay?"

"Yes." Cara nodded happily. Jericho nodded before getting up and getting redressed. When he was done, he bent over, picked up her clothes and handed them to her.

"You might want to take a hot shower; it will help with the soreness." Cara blushed as she raised herself into a sitting position and then frowned as he started gathering dishes and empty bottles.

"I will." She watched as he carried everything to the kitchen.

She then dressed as she heard running water, knowing he was doing the dishes. Cara was unsure of what to do, having never been in this position before. When Jericho reentered the room, she was still sitting on the couch waiting for him. She had royal blood in her veins and too much pride in herself to hide herself away in her room.

"I thought you were going to take a shower."

"I was hoping you might like to take one with me." Cara gave him what she hoped was a seductive smile, but having never given one before, she could not be sure.

"No, thanks, I have one in my room. I think I'll go to bed. I'll see you in the morning."

"Jericho..."

"Don't do this, Cara."

"Do what?"

"Have a postmortem of what happened."

"I don't understand." Cara tried not to be hurt at his attitude, but it was really hard when he was staring at her with such cold eyes.

"What's to understand? We had sex. It's over now, so like all men, I would like to go to sleep."

"Alone?"

"Yes, alone. I don't share my bed with anyone."

"Why?"

"Look, Cara, I really don't want to hurt your feelings, but I didn't want anything except sex. Now that the need has been taken care of, I'd like to go to bed."

Before he could continue on, Cara interrupted him. "So you got what you wanted, now you're done with me?" Desperately, Cara tried to keep the anger out of her voice.

"You're sounding more like a mortal woman by the minute. Cara, I gave you a good first time, and I made damn sure you got what you wanted. Something you can remember, hopefully with pleasure. But do I want to make it permanent or have sex with you again? The answer is no."

This time she couldn't keep the hurt out of her face. "Was I that bad?"

Cara was sure that people heard his sigh in town. "No, you weren't bad, just inexperienced. I prefer to have more experienced women." His voice took on a hard tone. "As soon as there is a room free at the hotel, I'll take you into town." He then turned to leave the room.

Cara was so angry she wanted to yell at him and storm out of the cabin, but she knew it was unrealistic. It was dark and late. She had never been stupid and didn't see any reason to start now, and that meant letting Jericho know she was no pushover.

"Just give me a ride into town in the morning. I'll find a place to stay. I don't need your help."

"Now you're just being plain silly. You're letting your hurt pride get the better of you."

"Don't speak to me as if I'm a child. I'll have you know

that I am quite a bit older than you."

"How much older?"

Cara had boxed herself in on that one, but she had every intention of being honest... kind of. "That would be hard to describe as time passes differently for immortals."

"Cut the bullshit."

Cara tried one more time to hold on to her temper, but his coldness was making it hard. He had stopped, gave her the choice and had made not one promise. The whole time they'd had sex, Jericho had never lost control. Even when he had climaxed, his facial expression never changed. It was her who had wanted and expected more from him. It was not Jericho's fault, but she was still pissed. Her body was still achy as if she had missed something.

"Run away, Jericho. I haven't asked one thing from you, other than maybe a repeat performance and even that was too much for you." She stood, glaring at his arrogant face.

A cruel laugh left his lips. "Like all women, if you don't want to answer a question, you strike out. You think my not wanting you again means you frighten me? In fact, you don't scare me at all, baby, whatever your real age. You simply don't interest me. I was horny and you were better than a hand job."

"You're crude."

He continued as if she hadn't spoken. "I'm tired and I am finished with this conversation. If you mean what you say, then you need to get to bed. I prefer you leave early in the morning." Jericho left without another word.

Cara swallowed around the lump lodged in her throat. She didn't want him to hear her crying. Instead, she went to her room and took off her clothes then cried in the shower where the running water prevented him from hearing her.

She was angry she had pushed him, but had been unable to stop herself. She had wanted him again and instead of tempting him, she had pushed him away. She had seen his past through Grimm's eyes and knew she must pull back, however she had never been one to run from a challenge.

How many arguments had she and Grimm had over souls? Each of those times that they had both been called, she had fought for the soul to have a second chance while Grimm disagreed. The soul would look at them in fear, knowing who they wanted to win, but more often than not, Grimm had won. That did not keep her from trying, though. If she could stand up to Grimm, she certainly could stand up to Jericho. However, for some reason, something inside Cara told her Jericho was the more dangerous adversary.

After Cara showered, she stood in her room. She wasn't tired. Seeing a television in the corner, she walked over to it and played with it until it turned on. Finding a control similar to the one Jericho had, she lay on the bed and fiddled with it until she successfully changed the channels. She was looking for another comedy, she needed a good laugh. She flipped another channel and a scene appeared on the screen.

Cara's mouth dropped open. Jericho had not shown her a movie like this earlier, thank goodness. Her face turned a bright red. The man and woman twisted around the bed. The woman was groaning in excitement, holding the man close, gripping his hips between impossibly long legs. It wasn't the woman who had Cara's attention, though, it was the man.

He wasn't as good looking as Jericho and his body definitely didn't compare, but what drew her attention were his movements. This man's face was tense with a sheen of sweat that covered his body and he trembled as much as the ecstatic woman. This man exhibited no control, just complete enjoyment in the woman he was thrusting within.

Jericho had never, at any time, looked like this while they'd had sex. Just the opposite, he never lost control once. Even when he had come inside her, she would never have known by his facial expression if she hadn't felt him stiffening beneath her. She meant no more to him than any other woman he had sex with.

Disheartened, Cara was about to turn the television off when the woman took control and really gave Cara an education in how to turn a man into a trembling mess. Cara grinned and made herself more comfortable on the bed. After all, a little education never hurt anyone.

* * *

Destiny stood gaping at her sister. "I can't believe you just did that."

Fate shrugged. "It's not as if I put the program on, I just gave her a nudge to turn the channel."

Destiny's eyes rounded even more as she watched Cara's movements before turning back to her sister.

"Oh, close your mouth Destiny. I just realized I may have protected Cara a little too much for her own good."

"So you put on porn for her." Her strangled voice was filled with laughter.

"Not porn, erotica, and I didn't put it on. As I said, it was already on."

Destiny nodded dumbly at her sister, "Yes, I can see the difference."

Fate gave a sinister smile. "I bet the next time he touches her, he won't walk away so easily."

Shocked, Destiny could only stare at Fate, realizing that even after all these centuries, her sister could still do the unexpected.

"If he's able to walk at all." Destiny burst out laughing, and for the first time since her daughter's disappearances, Fate smiled. She didn't laugh, but she came close.

Chapter Nine

Cara dressed as soon as the sun rose in the morning. It had been a long night and Cara had tossed and turned for most of it. When she heard Jericho leave his room, she opened her door and met him in the hallway.

He turned towards her, noticing that she looked like she hadn't slept. Jericho hardened himself against her. Obviously, he had made the right choice not to take her up on her offer of a second go around when she had trouble dealing with the first. Her feelings were hurt and he saw no reason to prolong her pain.

"Give me a couple of minutes to get my boots on. I'll meet you at the truck."

Cara nodded. Without a word and with her nose stuck in the air, she brushed passed him in the small hallway, put her coat on and went outside into the cool morning. The door clicked softly behind her with a click that said a thousand words.

Jericho gritted his teeth. He wanted to shake her silly. He was getting fed up with the injured, innocent act. She was damn lucky she hadn't provoked the side of him that she was tempting or she would have trouble sitting for a couple of days. The sooner he got rid of Cara, the better.

Cara walked over to the truck to wait, wishing she had thought to ask for the keys because she was beginning to shiver in the early morning air. Her body still hadn't acclimated to the change in environment. Out of the corner of her eye, Cara noticed a movement at the tree line surrounding the house. Curious, she turned, thinking it was her imagination, when she spotted a huge wolf running straight for her. Frightened, Cara turned to run, however the wolf was faster. Cara had the breath knocked from her when the wolf took a running jump at her and connected with her back.

The wolf lay on top of her as Cara heard loud explosions and glass shattering. When it moved to stand next to her, she rolled over on her back only to see the wolf running to the tree line, turning to growl back at her. Confused, Cara couldn't understand what was going on and sat up.

When she then turned toward the cabin, trying to get her shaky legs underneath her, Jericho flung the door open. He had obviously heard the commotion outside. Before he could move from the doorway, the wood frame next to his head shattered into pieces as a bullet struck it, which was when it finally dawned on Cara's dumbfounded mind that they were being shot at. She looked around to find the best cover she could and realized she was out in the open.

She scrambled to her feet and started to run towards Jericho, but when another shot burst out his front window, she realized she was only endangering him. Another growl let Cara know that the wolf had remained nearby, next to the trees. Instinct had her turning toward the animal as the shots now turned on her. The bullets shot dirt up as she ran for the trees.

She dimly heard Jericho yelling, but Cara didn't hesitate, she had to draw the shooter away from him. She didn't want him hurt because of her.

She ran harder towards the waiting wolf. When she reached him, he turned, running deeper into the woods, and Cara followed as fast as she could. The animal moved quickly, but her fear gave her speed, so it was several minutes before her body began to tire. As she slowed, barely able to keep up with the fast wolf, it turned to growl at her.

Gasping to catch her breath, she got a good look at the animal. It was huge with a dark brown coat.

It walked back to her and took the bottom of her jacket into his mouth and tugged at her. Given no choice, Cara once again started following the animal as he led her to a concealed cave. It was so overgrown with brush she would never have seen it, even from just a few feet away, if she hadn't seen with her own eyes when the animal disappeared behind the foliage.

It was dark inside and Cara began to doubt the wisdom of hiding with the wolf. The wolf began whining and Cara moved to stand next to it and then felt him take her coat in his jaws again, tugging her downward until she was sitting on her knees.

"I guess you want me to sit?" Cara asked, knowing the wolf would be unable to answer.

She felt the hard ground beneath her and put out a hand to find a more comfortable position. When she did, her hand brushed something. Blindly reaching out her fingertips, she found what she thought might be a lamp and her searching fingers soon found the matches lying next to it. It took a few minutes, but soon the cave was filled with a soft light.

It was a small cave, though tall. She had been able to stand without the roof of the cave coming near her head. There were boxes near the back of the cave and even sleeping bags. This was definitely someone's hideout with provisions for them to live awhile from what Cara could gather.

"Well what do we do now? Wait, or try to head back to

the cabin? Should I try to make it to town?"

The wolf only stared back at her.

Cara began shaking, the adrenaline rush was beginning to wear off and the cold ground was draining her energy. When her teeth began chattering, the wolf looked at her curiously before walking over to the sleeping bags, taking one in his jaws and dragging it closer to her side.

"You're a smart wolf." Cara unfolded the bag and wrapped it around herself. The warmth was instantaneous and she felt like crying in relief. It wasn't long before her eyes began to droop and she yawned several times, attempting to catch herself from falling asleep. She soon lost the battle and slid sideways, burrowing further into the warm bag. The wolf knew she had fallen asleep and moved to adjust the bag so that she was better covered. Then he sat back to wait.

He was curious as to how long it would take the human male Cara was staying with to find her. He had hidden her well. Only an extremely good tracker would find them and the man, Jericho, was no experienced tracker, however he did have a couple of advantages. One was his heritage, the other was his feelings for the woman. He had seen the man's face when he had discovered Cara was being shot at. The man hadn't liked it one bit. He had stormed from the porch before he saw Cara was running from him instead of to him. Fury had been in his face.

The girl was in deep trouble regardless of who found her.

He padded over to the sleeping woman, who bore no resemblance to her stubborn aunt, which was a good thing in his book. The wolf made a smile, if such was possible, and lay down close to the sleeping woman. After all, he wanted to provide her with all the warmth he could. How he wished he could see Destiny's face at this turn of events. He would bet she was furious and even now seeking to rectify this situation. The wolf laid his head on his front paws and closed his eyes. He was sure he wouldn't have to wait long.

* * *

Jericho moved silently through the quiet woods.

When he had come back out from the cabin with a rifle, he had caught a glimpse of a SUV driving from the cover of the trees. Hopefully the shooter had decided to leave, if not, then the maniac better stay out of his range. He wouldn't hesitate to use the rifle if Cara was in danger.

Jericho's mind still saw her running hell bent toward the trees. At first he couldn't understand why she had not run to the safety of the cabin. After thinking further, though, he knew why; he had seen her expression when the gunshot had almost hit him and that was when she had changed directions.

As he walked, he looked for signs of her passing through. Her trail wasn't hard to find. Her headlong flight had left several signs even he had no trouble reading. It took a good half-hour before all signs of her disappeared. He searched, but it was as if she had disappeared into thin air.

As he said the words to himself, a sudden, unnamed fear filled his stomach. What if the shooter had doubled back? What if her family had come for her? She had been unbelievably angry at him; would she leave without telling him, hoping a guilty conscience would bother him? The stupid woman must not have figured out that he didn't have a conscience.

He would continue to search until either he found her or there was evidence that she was no longer in the woods. He didn't know what time it was, but the sun was high in the sky; by his best guess, he had been there a couple of hours. He had gone quite a way from where he had lost her trail.

Jericho was about to search further down a slope, thinking maybe she had lost her balance, when a sudden wind pushed him back. The strength of the wind pulled at his clothes. When he tried to go forward against the wind, it picked up strength, tugging harder. It was as if a storm was blowing with a clear sky. Knowing the abilities of Cara's family, he decided to follow his intuition, so he turned in the direction the wind was tugging. As he felt the wind pushing him forward, he was sure he had made the right decision.

The wind led him deeper into the woods until a huge rock-covered hill blocked his path. One part was heavily covered with brush as the wind tore at the foliage. Frowning, he hunched down and saw that the brush pulled away from the rock and that there was an opening to a cave. The cave was on his property, but he had been unaware of its existence.

He crawled through the opening and sat back on his haunches in shock. Cara lay in a sleeping bag with a wolf standing beside her, who, when he saw Jericho raise the rifle to his shoulder, padded softly passed him and out of the cave. Jericho didn't know why he didn't pull the trigger other than he had felt no sense of danger from the animal. Still, relief flowed through his veins when he left without any trouble. He hadn't wanted to fire the rifle in the small confines of the cave.

He sat down next to the sleeping woman and noticed the dark circles under her eyes. With a shaking hand, he reached out to wake Cara, who immediately awoke with an expression of fear on her lovely face. The whole time Jericho had spent searching for her, he had not allowed his mind to focus on the feelings he was developing for this mysterious beauty, yet staring down into her face, he was struck by a tidal wave of fury and lust. Fury that she had run away to protect him and lust at the remembrance of the sex they had shared last night.

He had held back last night, knowing she had no experience, allowing her to set the pace. Today, Jericho realized that he wanted her again, except this time, her innocence wouldn't hold him back. She had wanted to have sex with him again last night and he had walked away.

Now, walking away was the last thing on his mind.

Jericho stood up and pulled his jacket off, laying the rifle within easy reach. Then he proceeded to remove his boots. He saw the drowsiness leave her eyes and desire replace it within their blue depths. He bent down and opened the sleeping bag, noticing she was still wearing her jacket. Roughly he removed it then her shirt and bra followed.

Cara felt like she was dealing with a different Jericho. Last night, everything about Jericho had been slow and gentle, almost detached. Today, it was as if he couldn't rid her of her clothes fast enough and there was nothing gentle about him. His normal, stoic expression was gone; his features drawn tight and fierce. Cara could see his Indian heritage and imagined that his ancestors were once feared. If Jericho was anything like them, then Cara could understand the terror that they had inspired.

He made her heart beat faster even knowing that he would never hurt her. She had a feeling his kid gloves were off, though. Thank goodness, Cara was tougher than she looked and she was more than his match. She came from a line of strong women who had never feared anything; in fact, it was others who feared them.

"You're not a virgin anymore." Jericho pulled off his shirt. Staring down into her eyes as he unbuttoned his jeans.

"No, I'm not." Cara raised her chin, refusing to be embarrassed.

"I won't be as easy on you as I was last night, even though I know you're still sore."

"I wanted you again last night. I still want you, Jericho."

He had removed his jeans and stood in front of her completely naked. Cara's breath caught in her throat. He was glorious. His bronze skin was highlighted by the dim light, giving him a pagan appearance.

"I want you to know that I don't have any diseases and

I can't get you pregnant. I had a vasectomy when I was nineteen."

Cara guessed that this conversation was a protocol between mortals before having sex.

"I don't have any diseases either. Now, are we through talking?" Cara hid her sadness that Jericho had voluntary destroyed any chance he had of becoming a father.

Cara let Jericho lay her down on the sleeping bag after sliding her jeans down her shaking thighs. She couldn't stop herself from trembling. The cave was cold and made goosebumps rise on her sensitized flesh, but Jericho did not let her feel the cold long. His body covered hers, his legs sliding intimately between her own, startling her as he immediately began making her ready for him.

His lips found hers in a kiss of exquisite fire that drew all thoughts of the cold from her. While his tongue thrust deep as his fingers delved within her, his other hand burrowed into her hair, tilting her head back to give him better access to her mouth. When she couldn't suppress her moans of want any longer, his lips found an already taut nipple, sucking it deep within his mouth before releasing it to gently bite her neck, leaving a red mark.

Cara was sure she couldn't stand his teasing any longer and pulled at his hair until he gave her what she wanted by returning to her aching breast and sucking the nipple deeper into his wet mouth. Before turning to give the other breast the same treatment, he placed another small bite on its peak, forcing a rush of liquid to escape her cunt.

Her hand slid down his taut stomach, marveling at the strength his body displayed. She investigated every glorious muscle as she slid her hand down to grip a buttock, pulling his hips closer, needing him desperately inside of her.

Jericho knew she was ready for him when she pulled him closer. He removed his damp fingers from her tight sheath and placed his cock at her moist entrance. This time, he didn't try to go slow, pumping his cock inside of her with hard, firm strokes, giving her little time to adjust.

Her moans of pleasure filled his mind as he pumped harder within her tight sheath. He looked down to see her biting her lip, so he leaned down and licked her lips until she started to hungrily return his kisses.

"I don't think I can take anymore, Jericho."

"Yes, you can." He didn't ask, he demanded. His strokes did not slow; instead, he raised her thighs until they now gripped his side tilting her hips upward at an angle to even further deepen his hard strokes.

"Jericho." Her voice had grown tight, hesitant.

"Are you my woman?"

Cara's head thrashed back and forth on the sleeping bag, her stomach muscles tensed, her hands lifted to brace themselves on his slick chest. She realized he was breathing heavily while his features blazed with a savage, pagan beauty. He showed every sign of a man being tortured by desire; none of these signs had been present last night. He had been gentle, easing her into sex. Now, the mask he always wore was removed, showing what he expected of a woman that could hold her own as his lover.

"Are you my woman?"

Cara understood what he was asking of her. To trust him to know that he would not hurt her, but would she accept him past her comfort zone? He was asking her to be what he needed.

"Yes." Cara's hand fell away to once again grip his buttocks and pull him closer within her tight depths.

"Then take all of me." With those words he stroked his cock even harder and further within her channel. Cara forced her tight muscles to relax and tilted her hips until she felt the full length of him sliding deep inside of her.

He took control of her body, showing her how he enjoyed sex; what he expected of her if she was woman enough to give him what he needed. He liked it hard and deep. In return, he gave her the fuck of a lifetime, one that she would remember with a smile and a drenched pussy.

Jericho's thumb played with her clit until its exposed

hood rested against his cock. With every movement, the friction caused a rush of wetness, which allowed him to slide within her at an even faster pace. Cara had always hoped that sex would be great, but this went beyond greatness. It was a pleasure so intense she wasn't sure she could stand it. The harder he pumped, the harder she wanted him.

The soreness in her pussy from last night left her tender, causing her to grip his cock tighter. She thought the small amount of pain would hinder her; instead, Cara was surprised at how it magnified her pleasure. Jericho could not go fast enough to suit her, so she started grinding her hips upward, meeting his strokes with a forcefulness of her own.

A series of hard thrusts had Jericho groaning and Cara screaming as their orgasms reached a peak neither had felt before. Cara saw the brief glint of surprise in Jericho's dark eyes before he lowered them.

This time, when he rolled off her, it wasn't to get dressed, but to pull her on top of him while grabbing the sleeping bag to cover them both.

When Cara looked down into his face, she did not see love or even affection on his face, yet what she did see brought a tender smile to her passion swollen lips. The air of detachment that always surrounded him was gone. What she saw was a man exhausted from pleasuring his woman. For all of Jericho's tough talk, he still had ensured that she had reached her peak before he had allowed himself to come.

Cara lay her head down on his shoulder and snuggled closer to his warmth. If he hadn't cared about her, he wouldn't have been concerned if she had been satisfied. Cara's hand traced softly across his tight stomach then lower until her fingers moved through the curls at the base of his cock before taking his still semi hard erection in her hand. His hand caught hers and moved it to his chest.

"Don't even think about it," Jericho grumped.

Cara smiled against his shoulder and wondered if he realized he had placed her hand over his heart.

* * *

Fate turned toward her sister. "Don't push it. You came close to interfering."

Destiny shrugged. "I couldn't resist the temptation."

"You've resisted until now. Don't let your hatred of Rocque lead you to make a stupid mistake."

Destiny turned away from the star-studded night to study Fate's features. "Is that a warning?"

Fate turned toward her sister and shrugged. "It's more than you gave me."

Chapter Ten

Thor sat at the head of the huge table and looked around him. His warriors were as bored as he. They had drunk enough ale that the minor offense of knocking a chalice of wine over had led to a free-for-all brawl. Benches were thrown and food went flying in the pandemonium. Thor had to find something to keep them busy soon or he wouldn't have a table sturdy enough to sit at. When one warrior pulled a hank of her opponent's hair out, leaving a bloody patch of scalp, he'd had enough.

"Cease this fighting and leave me." He did not have to raise his voice, he was immediately obeyed. As the warriors filed passed his chair, lustful looks were thrown towards him. The women were taking their boredom out in the bedroom. Working their frustrations out on him during sex had provided them with an outlet and him with a sore cock. He needed something to distract him and provide fresh meat for the Valkyrie.

Thor walked out to his stone balcony and called the one woman's name he had sworn never to utter. "Fate." He stared at the darkened sky. It wasn't long before the hair on the back of his neck rose.

"That didn't take long."

"I have been waiting for your permission to speak to you." Fate tried to keep the reprimand out of her voice, yet was unsuccessful.

Thor turned to face the powerful Moirae with a raised brow. Fate lowered her head in deference.

"My father asked me to give you an audience. Don't make me regret my decision. What is it you wish to speak to me about so urgently?"

"I humbly ask that you retrieve my daughters from the portals they were forced into when they were attacked."

Thor leaned back onto the balcony and looked at the woman's tired face. Thor couldn't remember when she had ever looked less than perfect. The worry about her daughters must be eating her alive because she was unable to help them.

"Why ask me? You know I would never do anything to help you. I think it is fitting that you have now lost the only things that held any importance in that cold heart of yours."

Fate's voice softened, "I love all my children."

"Tread carefully, Fate. I am in no mood for your games." Thor's face hardened further. Fate's heart nearly burst with pride. She had created this warrior and he was a sight to behold. His golden beauty was stamped with a male arrogance that merely enhanced the muscled body which only a Valkyrie was permitted to touch.

"I can understand you not wanting to help me, but, Thor, they are your sisters, and whether you want to admit it or not, you are the only one who can help them."

Thor turned once again to study the sky. As much as he really did not want to help his mother, he would not allow his sisters to be harmed. "Very well, I will go to Broni first. Her danger is more imminent than the others."

Thor started to gather the thunder in which he would travel when Fate's sharp voice stopped him. "No, you must first go after Cara. She must be returned here at once." Fate pointed to a portion of the sky that Thor had not noticed, a dark cloud was insidiously advancing towards Cara and was almost within reach of touching her.

Thor turned to look at Fate, surprise in his eyes. "I see why you are a master at your work, Fate. I did not see the threat advancing so quickly toward Cara. What about Broni?"

Fate stiffened her spine and ignored the ache in her heart at the pain Broni would have to brave, but she was her mother's daughter and she would survive, whereas if Cara wasn't helped soon, she would be beyond their reach forever.

"Broni would be the first to insist that you go after Cara. She will understand. I will provide her with what assistance I am allowed."

"Very well." Again Thor raised his hand to gather the thunder. As the lightning grew closer and the thunder louder, he turned to look at the woman who gave him birth. "I do this for my sisters, never for you. And know this, Fate, whatever deal you struck with my father, I will see that it is met."

"I agreed to Odin's demands. I will not go back on my word."

"What if she doesn't want to leave her human?"

"Kill him."

* * *

Cara and Jericho headed back to the cabin at nightfall. He kept her close as they walked through the forest, straining to listen for any sound that would betray an assailant waiting in the dark forest. When they reached the cabin, Jericho made her go through each room with him, not wanting to leave her alone as he searched.

"It's all right; whoever took that shot at you is gone. I didn't think they would be waiting for us here, but I wanted to make sure."

Cara shivered. "Do you think whomever it was will come back?"

Jericho gave her a hard stare. "You tell me? Whoever it was, they were shooting at you. Do you have any idea who it could be?"

Cara shook her head. "No, the one who tried to destroy my sisters and I was an immortal. Who shot at us today was obviously human. They want to hide their identity from those watching us and want their identity to remain secret. They know my family will retaliate as soon as they find out who tried to harm us."

"What do you mean, those watching us?" Jericho looked around the room as if they were surrounded by invisible entities.

Cara laughed at him. When he turned his cold expression back to her, she guessed he had no sense of humor. "No one is in the room with us, but my family can look at us from time to time. Sort of like your reality TV."

"Is there a way to turn it off?"

Cara couldn't help laughing once more. "No."

"Were they watching when we were having sex?" Again, he looked around the room as if he could see those watching them.

"There is an unspoken rule allowing us privacy at such times, but," Cara bit her lip to keep her laughter contained, "we do have the occasional voyeur."

"Tell them to cut it out."

Cara spread her hands out. "How do you propose I do that? I can no longer communicate with them."

"Well, think of something," Jericho ordered her.

Cara silently looked at him, noticing the faint blush that covered his cheeks. It was dawning on her that he was uncomfortable. "Are you embarrassed?"

"Why shouldn't I be? You just told me that several immortals are watching every move we make, including those of a private nature, and I am supposed to be okay with that? Can I ask what made you assume that I am an exhibitionist?"

Cara tried, she really did, but she couldn't hold her

laughter back any longer. She doubled over when his affronted expression became too much for her to bear.

"Well, I can see that you are in no mood to be reasonable, so I'm going to bed. If you're hungry, you can forage for yourself. Goodnight." He was almost out of the room before Cara could gather herself.

"You mean you are going to your room? But I thought…" This time it was Cara's turn to blush.

Jericho didn't even turn around, the arrogant jerk that he was simply kept walking out of the room. "Until you can figure a way to keep prying eyes away from my bare ass then our show has just been cancelled."

Jericho woke the next morning to the smell of frying bacon, and unless his twitching nose was mistaken, he also sniffed the odor of biscuits. He was thirty-five-years-old and had never woken to the smell of a cooking breakfast.

He pulled a soft pillow over his face, blocking out the smells. The inept girl was probably getting ready to burn down his cabin. The food couldn't possibly taste as good as it smelled. She was taking over his cabin as if she was going to be staying, as if she belonged. He was going to set her straight. Right after he tried her breakfast.

Cara fumbled with the frying pan, wincing as the popping grease struck her hands. The cooking show hadn't shown that there was going to be popping grease. If they were going to give a cooking demonstration, then they at least should be accurate, you would think. Especially if it could involve the possibility of pain.

"Darn it!" The pan slid crazily as she tried to maneuver it off the hot burner.

"Having problems?" Cara looked up to find Jericho standing in the doorway.

He had expected a mess; to see flour strewn everywhere and burnt food. Instead, the table had a platter of biscuits waiting, a heaping bowl of scrambled eggs and the bacon was sitting on the counter. She had also set the table with plates and silverware. Beside each plate sat a glass of orange juice. Jericho felt his throat tightening.

"How did you do all this?"

Cara gave him a cheeky grin. "Did you know that there is a TV channel that shows you how to cook?"

"No, I didn't."

"Have a seat. It's all ready." Cara smiled at him. He could see the flush of accomplishment on her pretty face. There was no way he was going to sit at that table.

"No, thanks. I'm not hungry." He turned to leave the kitchen.

"I don't understand. You have to be hungry since you haven't eaten since yesterday." The smile was leaving her face and hurt was entering her eyes.

"When I get hungry, I'll fix myself a sandwich."

"So it's because I fixed this food that you don't want it?" Cara's confusion had Jericho almost ready to relent until his eyes found the small glass of flowers she had set on the table.

Angry, Jericho pointed to the table. "Why did you do all this?"

Her confusion deepened as he took a step back from the table. Cara stared at the table that was making him so angry. "I thought you might be hungry."

"No, that's not why you did it." He looked at her with fury in his eyes. "You are trying to make more out of this than there is."

"More out of what?"

"Us. What you may believe happened yesterday in the cave. You are trying to find a place here as if you're going to stay. As if you think we are a couple now with all the happily ever after bullshit."

"And my cooking breakfast says all that?" Cara watched as he nodded his head.

She turned off the stove and moved towards him, noticing how his eyes slid down her body. She hadn't bothered to dress. Her body had seemed to finally become acclimated to the environment and she had simply cooked in the t-shirt she had put on to sleep in. The thin white shirt only came to the tops of her thighs and showed that she wore no underwear. He took a step back as she stalked toward him.

"So we're not a couple, but it was you who wanted to know if I was your woman yesterday. What was that?"

Jericho shrugged. "It was a moment of adrenaline, us responding to the danger around us."

"That was it? So, let me get this straight. You want to fuck me when you want to with no strings attached?"

Anger darkened his eyes. "It's called friends with benefits."

"Well, I'm learning all kinds of useful information from you, Jericho. I just can't express my gratitude at you guidance."

Jericho tried not to notice how her breasts strained against the thin t-shirt. How her anger was making her breasts jiggle with her quickened breathing. His hands clenched into fists to keep himself from grabbing the firm mounds of flesh.

He watched as she turned to walk over to the pretty table she had set. "And since you don't want to eat the breakfast I cooked because I might misinterpret what it means, let's see if you can figure out what this means." With the speed of a striking snake, she picked up a glass of the orange juice and flung the cold contents into his face.

Stunned, Jericho was motionless for a second until he saw her reach for the bowl of scrambled eggs. Quickly, he moved forward until he could reach her arm holding the eggs. "Put them down," he ordered.

"My pleasure." With a twist of her fingers, she let the eggs slip out of her hand. The bowl with the hot eggs landed on his bare feet.

"Damn, that hurt."

"Good." Cara moved to grab the biscuits.

"Stop it, Cara!" Jericho tried to stop her, but slid in the eggs, barely managing to catch himself from falling on the floor by grabbing the edge of the table for balance. Cara helped by pushing his head forward into the platter of biscuits. Not content with only doing that, she used all her strength while he was off balance to smash his face into them.

"Cut it out!" Jericho finally managed to get his balance in the slippery mess, barely able to breathe. He also managed to extradite himself from the enraged woman's hands. "Have you lost your mind?"

"Yes, and you have driven me to it, you idiot!" Still not content with the damage she had inflicted upon him, Cara moved in on him again. Jericho had enough sense to know when to get the hell out of dodge and this was it. He moved to slide by the enraged woman, but she blocked his exit. This wasn't going to be pretty.

Jericho tried tact. "Look, Cara, maybe I was wrong and read more into the situation than there was. I'm sorry." Jericho got nervous when he saw the calculating smile begin to curl her luscious lips.

"You weren't mistaken Jericho, in fact you were right. I was trying to do what normal couples do on a Sunday morning, and if you're trying to keep me from caring about you, then you're too late. You see, I have fallen in love with you and no matter how much of a jackass you show yourself to be won't change that fact."

"You don't love me."

"Yes, I do."

"No, you don't."

"Jericho, no matter how many times you deny it, you won't change my feelings."

This time Jericho didn't let her stop him from leaving the room; he pushed passed her. Cara doggedly followed him down the hall. When he went into his room and slammed the door behind him, she followed. Jericho was jerking his egg stained jeans down his hips while Cara admired his firm ass while she also couldn't help staring at his cock straining upwards. He may be furious with her, but he wanted her badly. She didn't miss the small gleam of moisture clinging to the crest.

"Get out!"

"No, I'm not going anywhere."

This time her words let loose a storm of fury within him. Cara could see it overtake him. His eyes darkened until they were almost black, and his muscles tightened until she thought they would surely burst from his arms. Jerking his shirt off before throwing it down on the floor, the loosened crumbs of her biscuits fell at Jericho's feet.

Cara tried not to laugh at him, she really did, but the big, bad Indian staring back at her, looking as if he had a serious case of dandruff, did her in.

He grabbed her and pushed her up against the door. One hand buried itself in her hair, straining her neck back until she was looking into his stoic expression. He had trampled his fury down so all that was left was a coldness that Cara did not know if she would be able to reach.

"If you want to play rough, then you came to the right man. If you can dish it out, then you had better be damn prepared to handle it." Crudely he ground himself against her, forcing her legs to part and allowing him to plaster himself closer to her.

"I can handle anything you give me." Cara didn't flinch from him, knowing that was what he expected of her.

If she wanted Jericho, then she had to prove to both of them that she was more than a match for him. He was a warrior, he had fought his whole life for survival, and he wouldn't tolerate less from the woman that would finally win his heart. Cara had every intention of being that woman, whether Jericho knew it or not.

"Let's just see, shall we." His mocking tone left Cara in no doubt that he believed she would call a halt when things got too hot. Well, he was in for a surprise. She happened to want him as bad as he wanted her. His hand slid the shirt up her soft thighs, going immediately to grasp her wet heat, a finger plunged into her. Using a knee, he forced her legs wider so that he could move further within her.

"Jericho..." Cara could not help moaning his name. She wanted him unbelievably bad. It seemed that most of the time since she met him was spent wanting him. She ground her head back against the door.

"You're hot for me, aren't you?" he whispered into her ear, making her shiver. His finger began to move quicker and harder within her, making her hips thrust forward as each stroke sent flames of desire burning higher until she thought she would burst. Jericho wouldn't allow her release, though; he stilled his finger until her body pulled back from the edge of the climax he had brought her to. Cara couldn't keep the whimpers of need from escaping.

Jericho eased away from her body until he could work the t-shirt up her waist and over her breasts. He immediately sucked a nipple into his waiting lips, suckling and nibbling until he saw that it had gone from a pale pink to a red before he moved to its twin.

Cara couldn't keep her hips still. Desperately, she tried to grind herself against the thigh between hers, but he wouldn't let her, moving it away. Cara felt the heat of his cock as it strained against her belly, she tried to reach for it, to put it exactly where she wanted it, but Jericho jerked her hand away, pulling it behind her back. Using the grip he had kept in her hair, he pulled her away from the door. Cara thought he would lead her to the bed, but the warrior in him didn't have that necessity in mind.

"Get down on your knees." His guttural voice shocked Cara. Though his face remained expressionless, his voice gave his desire away.

Cara let herself go to the floor where a braided rug protected her knees from the hardwood floor. Jericho followed her until he covered her back. His lips buried themselves in her sensitive neck while his strong hands pulled her thighs apart until he was between them, his cock at her entrance. Another whimper left her lips as he nudged at her wetness, yet did not enter.

"Jericho, please, please fuck me." Cara didn't care that she begged him. She wanted him to know how desperately she wanted him.

"Oh, I'm going to fuck you, when you beg me to."

"I'm begging! I'm begging!"

"Not hard enough." His lips picked a patch of skin and began to nibble at the same time his hands held Cara in place and, when she tried to reach back to touch his cock, he once again grabbed her hand.

"No, you don't." He rose up slightly, pulling her t-shirt over her head without allowing her arms to slide free. He maneuvered the garment until it circled both wrists now bound behind her back. He moved forward again until her forehead touched the rug. She was completely open and helpless.

"I'm going to teach you a new phrase," he said with another seductive murmur in her ear.

"You are?"

"Yes, I am. Would you like to know what it is?"

Cara's newfound sexual confidence began to stutter at the sexual domination he was exhibiting. "I don't think so."

"How about I just show you?" With that sinister tone in his voice, Cara didn't know if she wanted him to show her anything. She felt him moving down her back, his lips grazing her spine. When he lingered at the small of her back, searching the small crevice with a slow lick of his tongue, Cara knew she was in trouble.

"Jericho…" He ignored her.

She felt his hands as they spread the cheeks of her buttocks. His lips lowered, following the crease that he had exposed. Cara tried to rise, but one hand pushed her back down until her forehead was once again on the rug. Jericho's tongue found the rim of her anus and nibbled until she thought that her lungs would burst with the need for oxygen.

Just when she thought she couldn't take another second, his lips slid lower until they reached the weeping wetness they were searching for. One second he was licking, the next his tongue was buried as far as it would go within her before he would draw it out just to plunge it inside once again while his fingers were busy rubbing her clit. She ached to climax, but every time she stiffened to, he pulled back to nibble at her anus until she was a withering mess, held up only by his hands on her hips.

"Please let me come, Jericho... please... please..." Again, he ignored her. Each time he pulled her back, he would once again delve into her slick cunt. Sweat dripped down her body as the torture he imposed on her continued. There was no area of her body that he didn't tease and taunt until Cara could not take it and her screams filled the bedroom.

It was only when she began to cry that he swiftly rose up between her thighs, circled her waist with a hard arm and pulled her hips up until her knees no longer touched the floor. He then took his cock and placed it at her entrance, sliding just the tip into her wetness; lubricating himself, moving closer, poised to enter her. Sobs were now tearing through her chest. She felt him removing the shirt from her wrists until they fell to her sides and he once again covered her back as he also let her knees touch the floor.

"Open for me." Cara knew what he wanted. She moved her hand, sliding it down her quivering belly until she touched herself. Using her fingertips, she parted herself, feeling his cock waiting. This time, she knew not to try to touch him. She was rewarded by finally feeling him stroke within her.

Quickly, Cara braced herself, placing her hands on the rug as he bent over her, pushing every massive inch of his penis within her tight channel. He wasn't gentle, no one could say Jericho was a gentle lover, but what he did was give her what she desperately needed. A hard, pounding that drove every inch of him inside her over and over again. Just when she thought that she could not possibly take him deeper, he pushed her thighs wider and gave her another inch. The force he was fucking her with made her slide across the rug. His hands left her hips to hold onto her shoulders, holding her still.

"Do you still love me?" his voice hissed out between his gritted teeth.

"Yes, Jericho! Yes!"

Her answer stopped him mid stroke until, with a curse, he levered himself off her.

"Jericho, please, I can't bear anymore."

He rolled Cara to her back then sat back on his knees, pulled her toward him until she was once again impaled on his cock, and entered her with one long, hard stroke. Tears leaked out of her eyes as he pounded within her, his fingers rubbing her clit.

Jericho watched as his cock slid in and out of her slick cunt. When he felt her muscles spasm with the beginning of her climax, he took his slickened finger and thrust quickly through her anal ring, finger fucking her ass. Cara screamed at the unbelievable pleasure he wrung from her. The climax that had begun spiraled even higher with a force that had every muscle in her body jerking. When he felt Cara's contractions easing, Jericho allowed himself to bury himself to the hilt, taking her hips in his hands and tilting her pelvis until he could fuck her as long and hard as he needed to reach his climax. When he felt Cara trying to struggle away from him, he held her still, never missing a thrust.

"Jericho, I can't take anymore." Cara felt as if her cunt was on fire; tight and raw from his hard pounding. The man was a fucking machine.

"Yes, you can. I need more." Jericho stared down into Cara's eyes. Understanding, Cara ground her hips back against his, fucking him as hard as he wanted. The pain burning in her pussy lightened as her excitement grew at trying to make Jericho lose control. Cara heard him groaning as he tried not to come. She knew he was enjoying fucking her tight cunt.

"Give it to me, Jericho, harder." As soon as the words left her lips, she felt Jericho thrust high within her, reaching to her womb. Cara felt her body explode in another climax that turned her world black as Jericho flooded her with his come.

His cock was still twitching when he pulled his penis from her and rose to his feet. He stood staring down at her. Cara looked up at the man who stood above her and didn't move. She could imagine how she looked, naked and sprawled on the braided rug with his semen still on her thighs. Yet she didn't move or cover herself and raised her chin proudly, staring back at him with all her love plain for him to see.

Pain flickered in his eyes so fleetingly that Cara would have missed it if she hadn't known about his past.

"Damn you."

"I love you, and no matter how hard you fuck me or how much you curse me, I'll still love you. In fact, one I enjoy wholeheartedly, the other I can put up with." Cara wiggled her ass on the rug and let her legs spread wider to let him know which one she had enjoyed. All modesty Cara determinedly suppressed, she had to prove to show him her love was real.

"You can't love me. We've known each other, what? A total of three days? You can't love someone you don't know."

"Now, that's where your wrong, lover. I know every tiny thing about you. I have ever since Grimm touched you that day at the restaurant, just as you know me." Cara saw the widening of his eyes and laughed mockingly at him. "You honestly can't believe that he would show you my life without returning the favor? He showed me everything."

"Be quiet." Rage, hot and heavy was plain on his face.

"He showed me a beautiful, little, lost boy whose soul was so pure it was white. You glowed."

"Stop!" Jericho yelled, trying to drown out her voice as if his life was a movie playing out in her mind.

Sadly, with tears in her eyes, Cara raised herself to a sitting position, knowing it was now or never.

"Then one day that monster entered your life and your soul began to die. She tortured you in every way imaginable. She pretended to home school you, so you were given no reprieve from the vicious bitch. She wanted to keep you dumb and subservient, but she couldn't break your spirit, could she, Jericho? When her and that spineless husband left the house, they locked you in a cage made for animals so you could not escape." Jericho stood still, her words bringing back memories he swore never to revisit. His muscled body began to shake and he broke out in a cold sweat.

"Her abuse was degrading and sick." Cara moved closer to him, her hand gently rising to rest on his muscular thigh. "I know why you have never allowed another woman since to touch you or put her mouth on your penis, but you grew older and stronger. She could no longer hold you down or turn your body against you, so she brought another young boy home to abuse. She thought she had broken you, that you would stand back and watch, but she underestimated you, didn't she, my warrior? Your fury broke loose and you took her neck in your hands and strangled her."

Tears slid down her cheeks at the soul she saw ravaged before her. She still heard the screams of the small child that Jericho had saved from the demented woman. She leaned against his thigh and laid her cheek against him. "The husband knew you were going to kill him and managed to call the police before you nearly beat him to death. When they arrived, he lied, said that it was you who had tried to harm the boy and when the woman had tried to stop you, you killed her. They believed him, the boy was in shock and unable tell what had happened. You didn't even try to defend yourself."

"They wouldn't have believed me, I could tell by their eyes. By that point, I no longer cared what happened to me." Jericho's emotionless voice drew her eyes upwards to him, letting him know he no longer shared those painful memories alone.

"But you cared later, didn't you? When they put you in prison with men twice your age and you had to fight just to survive those nights. You spent months in that prison before the boy was well enough to tell everyone the truth and gain your release. They tried to place you in another home, but you ran. You ran to this mountain and found your home."

"The Indian council gave me this land and made the government declare me an emancipated minor. They even helped me get my GED and help me find my job in construction." Jericho tried to move away from her, relieved she would finally shut up and leave him in peace, but she refused to release his leg. Jericho looked down at her to find that tears were still pouring from her eyes.

"Don't cry for me." He couldn't help how harsh he sounded. He damn sure did not want her pity.

"I'm not crying for you, I am crying for a child that no longer exists. Destroyed by a woman whose magnitude of evil I have rarely seen and, Jericho, I have lived a long time." Lifting a trembling hand she brushed the tears away until they glistened on her fingertips. "They show the anger I feel for a woman I consider less than human who owes me a debt that will never be repaid. That bitch stole something that was mine."

Jericho didn't want to know, but couldn't help asking. "What did she take?"

"Your heart."

Cara raised herself onto her knees and slid her hand up his body slowly. Her touch was feather light, loving, as she delicately touched his penis for the barest instant before moving to the dense black hair at its base. Her hand sought and traced each of his abs before raising herself to place a tiny kiss on each of his hips. She worshiped with each gentle touch and kiss. Cara's hands finally reached the area of his body she searched for. Her palm curved over his chest as if she was indeed able to hold his heart in her hand. She felt the steady rhythm of it beating beneath the bronzed flesh.

Jericho tried, he really did, but he looked down in surprise as his hand reached out and his thumb smoothed away her remaining tears. "And that matters so much to you, why?"

The horror of his childhood prevented him from becoming emotionally involved with anyone. The only way he had survived the violence was to bury his feelings until they no longer existed, yet her tears were proving to be a balm to the scars that remained and her next words made him wish for the impossible.

Softly, she whispered, "Because you would have loved me."

His voice thickened as he asked, "Are you so sure about that?"

Cara nodded and a glimmer of a smile found her trembling lips. "Yes, I'm very loveable."

"I can see that."

Jericho looked down at the brave woman who had bared her soul to him. He did the only thing he was capable of doing in that moment. He reached down and picked her up into his arms.

"What are you doing?"

"Carrying you to bed."

Chapter Eleven

"You made this mess, you get to clean it up." Jericho and Cara stared at the disaster in the kitchen.

"All right." Cara wasn't going to argue. She had enjoyed the afternoon of loving that the mess had brought about.

Jericho smiled at the happy woman. He could feel himself lowering his guard toward her and thought to break the moment, but couldn't bear to see the happiness leave her face just yet. He knew he was not able to give her the love she wanted returned, however that was something she would have to find out for herself.

"Come on, I'll help." They set out to clean the kitchen when they heard a knock at the front door.

"Stay here."

"I'm coming with you," Cara said. When she saw Jericho was about to argue, she interrupted, "The shooter from yesterday isn't stupid enough to come knocking on the door."

Jericho shrugged, knowing from the look in her eye she had no intention of listening to him.

Cara followed closely on Jericho's heels as he went toward the door. They were within several inches when a familiar voice rang out.

"Jericho, it's me, Billy."

Cara looked at Jericho in surprise as he opened the door. A smiling Billy stared back at the both of them.

"I'm glad to see you're okay, Cara." Cara took a step back, unable to alert Jericho without Billy knowing. "Aren't you going to invite me in?" Jericho took a step back, letting him enter before closing the door behind him. Cara felt panic rising in her throat. Billy was different. The color of his soul was murky, not black, but a blend of grays and mauves. Also, his mother's ghost was no longer with him.

Billy walked into the living room, staring at Cara while Jericho followed him. Cara tried to catch Jericho's eye, but he wasn't looking at her, instead he was looking at Billy with a frown on his face.

"What are you doing here?" Jericho asked.

"Why, I'm here to take Cara off your hands since I dumped her on you. I finally managed to slip away from that small town hick sheriff." Billy gave them an insincere smile.

Jericho stiffened. "You should have called first. You've wasted a trip out here. Cara will be staying with me." Jericho pulled Cara close to his side, leaving his arm around her waist, staking his claim before the younger man.

Billy shrugged. "I was afraid of that. She is beautiful and hard to resist, even for a hardass like you."

Jericho didn't smile. "I'm glad you understand."

Billy's laughter was as fake as the smile plastered on his lips. Cara could only hope that Jericho could see that something was off with Billy.

"Well, since I came all this way for nothing, how about offering me a cup of coffee before I head on the long trip home."

"Of course." Jericho motioned for Billy to head for the kitchen.

"What in the fuck happened in here?" Billy looked at the disaster area with eggs and juice on the slippery floor.

"We had a little bit of an accident," Cara murmured with a blush.

"I can see that. It looks like a tornado hit the room."

"One did," Jericho said wryly. "Cara, why don't you make the coffee while I try to clean a place for us to sit down?"

"That won't be necessary." Cara looked in dread as Billy pulled a handgun from his jacket pocket. Looking out of the corner of her eye, Cara could see that Jericho did not seem to be shocked at this turn of events. Billy pointed the gun towards her, placing his finger on the trigger.

Again, out of the corner of her eye, Cara saw a doorway open and Grimm enter the room. His stern visage gave no clue as to who he was here for. She knew he would be unable to help. He had been dispatched to collect a soul. Which one, was as yet unknown to everyone except Grimm.

Cara felt her throat tighten in fear. For the first time, she could truly feel the fear that those she had came to escort feel. Even knowing what awaited her, it was still terrifying. Would there be pain? Would it be quick? She also knew that she didn't want to leave Jericho. She had just found him and did not want to leave him. Sudden terror filled her heart with the sudden realization that he meant to kill Jericho also.

"Billy, why would you want to harm Cara when you went to so much trouble to keep her safe?" Jericho was hoping to distract the man until he had an opening to grab the gun. He had also seen Grimm's sudden entrance into the room.

"I think I can answer that question. He's had a spell placed on him. Whoever has done this is powerful enough to remove his mother's protection."

"I do not need any protection. My master has punished me for failing yesterday, but he will see I will not fail again.

I will be rewarded for your death."

Sadly, Cara shook her head. "No, Billy, you must understand. Once you have taken a life, there is no going back. You don't want to do this. I know your soul is filled with a kindness and gentleness I have rarely seen. You can fight the spell placed on you. Try, Billy, please. I would not want to see your soul destroyed because of another's malice."

"Shut up. I was warned you would try to sweet talk me out of killing you."

"Who warned you, Billy?" Cara desperately tried to gain any information she could, not only for her own safety, but her sisters' as well. She couldn't believe the same sweet man who saved her life the night she had become mortal was the same man who had deliberately hidden in the woods and tried in cold blood to shoot her and Jericho.

Billy shook his head. "I'm not telling you a damn thing." He saw Jericho make a sudden move toward him and pointed the gun toward him.

"No!" Cara screamed as Jericho reached and grabbed the gun, jerking it upwards just as it let out an explosion of sound.

The two men began to struggle in the slimy mess on the floor, which made it hard for them to stay upright. They fell with a crash, knocking over the table. Billy was beneath Jericho and his hand with the gun was pinned in a hard grasp by Jericho. Cara saw the muzzle of the gun turn towards Jericho and knew what she had to do. Reaching blindly behind her, she grabbed the first thing she could and rushed forward. Bending down while dodging thrashing arms and legs, Cara brought the heavy frying pan down on Billy's skull.

Billy went limp and Jericho tore the gun away from his now unresisting hand. He got to his feet, not taking his eyes off the unconscious man.

Both of them stood staring down at Billy, unable to

believe how close he had come to killing them.

Grimm moved forward, turning their attention to him.

She gave him a relieved smile. "I'm sorry, you'll be leaving alone."

Grimm shook his head. "You know better than that, Cara. Once dispatched, we always have a soul to collect."

"But I'm fine." She quickly inspected Jericho when it finally dawned on her who Grimm was there for.

Everyone turned to look at Billy who lay unmoving on the floor. He was not unconscious, he was dead. Cara's heart broke; she had taken a life. She began to cry as she thought of the sweet boy who had been so kind to her when she had needed help.

Grimm nodded as Cara noticed a dark glow move beside him. A doorway behind them opened as Grimm and Billy's spirit turned to enter the doorway.

"Grimm, please, ask him who sent him here to kill me."

Grimm turned to the dark glow. They couldn't hear them speaking, finally Grimm turned back to them and shook his head. "He doesn't know, only that it was a woman. She wore a cape that covered her body."

Grimm bent down to the still body and lifted it into his arms.

"What are you doing?"

"His life was taken because an immortal interfered. I can try to repair the damage someone else has done."

"Thank you, Grimm."

Grimm nodded. "Good luck, Cara. Be careful, little one. I miss having you around." He gave her a smile before turning once again to the dark glow. Both moved toward a doorway that opened as they walked closer. Grimm gave a final wave as they disappeared within.

Jericho turned to Cara. "What will happen?"

Cara began to shake. "I don't know. We can't return a life once it is taken, but Grimm will find a way if anyone can. He's very determined when he sets his mind to something. We have had many fights over a soul. I was never able to save a soul from him."

Jericho's arms surrounded her shaking body, trying to share his warmth. It was hitting her hard that she had been responsible for a death, even though she had saved his life. Billy had shown an abnormal strength and Jericho didn't know how much longer he could have held him off.

"You go lie down and I'll clean the kitchen."

"No, I want to help."

Jericho started to argue, but ultimately thought it would probably help take her mind off Billy and who was trying to kill her.

They set to work and got the kitchen cleaned in little time. To cheer Cara up, he made her favorite for dinner.

"You think spaghetti is going to make me feel better?"

"Is it working?"

Cara laughed. "Yes, it is actually. It just scares me to think that someone wants us dead so badly. I worry for Zerina and Broni; they are all alone. I was lucky I had you." Cara sent him a soft smile.

Jericho felt his throat tighten in fear. He didn't want her to depend on him. He didn't want her soft smiles or the love shining out of her beautiful eyes. His chair scraped back from the table and he started to rise from his chair to leave the room, to get the hell away from the feelings he fought against. A hurt look entered Cara's eyes, she knew he was about to run, and she wasn't going to say anything. She understood and she was going to let him go.

Jericho felt a gentle hand on his shoulder. When he turned, he didn't see anything, but he still felt the touch on his shoulder. As if it was telling him to stay, as if he left the table, there would be no going back. Jericho felt as if he was at a crossroads between his old, lonely life and a new one filled with love. With Cara.

He broke out in a cold sweat and began to shake. The imaginary hand tightened on his shoulder, giving him strength. He had built his physical strength so that he would always be able to protect himself, but he had ignored his heart. It was weak, afraid to trust and love. He didn't know how to be with someone day after day. He wasn't sure he could do it. To have someone around constantly wanting to be with him. Someone who could take away the loneliness and the pain of his past. If he just could be strong enough to let Cara love him.

"Would you like some more bread?" Cara shook her head. Not mentioning that there was plenty on the table.

"Okay." He nodded his head, and scooted his chair back under the table and then added more spaghetti to his plate.

Cara looked down at her plate and tried not to cry. She knew how hard it was for Jericho not to run. She was going to have to go slow with this man of hers. He was skittish and afraid of her feelings for him, however there was one lesson her father had taught that she was going to take to heart.

"What are you thinking about?"

Cara looked up, smiling. "Patience is a virtue."

Chapter Twelve

"You cheated!" Jericho accused.

"I did not." Cara tried to keep a straight face, but was unable to hold back her giggles.

Cara stared at the shirtless Jericho seated at the kitchen table and tried to look innocent, which was hard to do when she was guilty as hell. Who could blame her with the body the man had? When he had taught her poker, she had easily learned the game, but had become bored. Sensing her apathy, Jarrod raised the stakes and taught her strip poker; boredom was the last thing on her mind. Since he was the better player, she had learned to become devious.

"You did, I saw you pick up an extra card and hide another. You're not even a good cheater." Jericho gave her a disdainful look.

Cara gave him what she hoped was a sexy look.

"Are you sick?"

"No, I was trying to give you a sexy look."

"Baby, all you had to do to accomplish that was to let me win. There's nothing sexier than you naked."

"Yes there is, you naked."

He leaned back in his chair until it rested on only the

back two legs. "If you wanted me naked, all you had to do was ask."

Cara smiled at his easy teasing. The last week she had fallen even more in love with this man. He had become everything she had ever dreamed about in a lover. He made her hot merely by staring at him, shirtless with his faded jeans hugging his lean hips; Cara was amazed at how relaxed he looked. He had slowly let down his guard and let her in. His soul was just as dark as before, that couldn't change, but the hardness in his eyes and expression was gone. He made her feel special, that she was loved, whether he would admit it or not.

"Have you heard the phrase cheaters never prosper?" Leaning back further in the chair, he gave her a hard stare. "You seek to cheat the Indian? At one time your hair would have been prized. You might even have been taken captive and made to become my woman."

Cara's interest perked up. "Would you have punished me?"

"Definitely. Come here." The look he gave her had her instantly rising from her chair and walking slowly toward him.

"I don't know if I should, you look big and bad. Mean, too."

Jericho reached out and snagged one of her hands, pulling her towards him, letting the chair down until it rested on all its legs. Pulling her forward despite her playful resistance until she was straddling his lap, Cara settled herself on his lap in mock fear. She had lost her pants and panties in their poker game, so her bare butt nestled against his jean covered cock.

He gave her an arrogant look that would have done his ancestors proud and made her even wetter.

"I am big, but you are the one who's been bad. Very bad." Jericho placed his hand on her wiggling hips, holding her still. "Take off your top," Jericho ordered. Cara quickly shed her shirt and dropped it on the floor. "Now your bra." Her bra soon followed her shirt. "Kiss me." With each arrogant command, Cara felt a rush of liquid between her thighs.

She leaned forward until her bare breasts rested against his chest. Her nipples tightened at the contact. Cara put her hands in Jericho's dark hair and tugged his head down until she could reach his lips. She traced them with her tongue, but he refused to let her tongue enter his mouth. He was going to make her work for it. She could do that.

Cara rubbed her breasts against his chest and slowly began to rock her hips against his crotch, all the while, her lips teased at his lips with little nips. When he still refused to open to her, she raised her hand and placed it on his strong jaw, applying pressure until his mouth finally parted to admit her tongue. Cara explored the depths of Jericho's mouth as if savoring a fine wine and became lost in the pleasure of having him under her control. That was until he began to respond and showed her that she was still an amateur compared to him.

His mouth became demanding as his tongue began dueling with hers, entering her mouth and forcing her head back until his hand tangled in her hair to hold her still. His hand raised and traced a nipple before releasing her mouth and pulling her further back until her back was arched and her breasts were thrusting upwards. His lips covered one rosy nipple, sucking hard until Cara thought she would scream in ecstasy. Then he caught the nipple between his teeth giving it a gentle bite.

"Do that again," Cara begged.

Jericho's lips switched to her other breast, sucking strongly. Cara tensed on his lap, waiting for the small bite of pain he would inflict on her nipple. The longer he made her wait, the more sensitive she became until, when he finally bit her, she screamed as an orgasm took her by surprise.

One of Jericho's hands went to her crotch, rubbing until her head fell forward weakly on his chest. She trembled as she lay against him, rubbing her cheek against his bare chest. With a hand still buried in her hair, he pulled until she looked up at him. His harsh features showed his Indian heritage. For an instant, Cara did feel as if she were his captive.

"I want you." A tear slid down her cheek. Cara knew in her heart what Jericho was unable to bring himself to admit.

"I love you." She gave him the words he needed to hear, to believe in the deepest recesses of his bruised heart.

Jericho rose from the chair with her legs still wrapped around his waist.

"Let's go to bed." Cara laid her head on his shoulder.

"Only if you promise to ravish me." A deep chuckle was her response.

"I think I can promise that." In one movement he removed her legs from his waist and flipped her until she was now lying on his shoulder. Giggling, Cara didn't know which she looked forward to more, her impending ravishment or the orgasm that was going to rock her world. Then Cara realized it was a win, win situation.

Later, Cara lay across Jericho's chest, not wanting to wake him as she silently slid from underneath his arm. Finding her clothes strewn around the room, she picked them up and placed them in a basket before gathering fresh ones and heading to the shower.

She enjoyed the hot shower as it soothed her aching body, grinning at the memories of what had brought about the pleasurable aches. She dressed in jeans and one of Jericho's t-shirts before reentering the bedroom. She debated waking Jericho, but decided not to. The poor man needed his rest; she had plans for later that night.

Frowning, Cara walked to the bedroom window. It was getting dark outside hours before sundown. Thinking that a storm was approaching, she looked out the window. What she saw terrified her. Running back to the bed, she shook Jericho, who woke immediately.

"We have to get out of here!"

He didn't waste any precious time. Jumping out of the bed, he grabbed his jeans and pulled them on. Cara handed him his shirt and shoes.

"What's wrong?"

"There's an eclipse."

He finished putting on his shoes and frowned at her. "That's nothing to worry about."

Hurriedly, Cara explained, "An eclipse is the only time when your world is invisible to ours. Whoever is trying to kill us will remain unseen by my mother and aunt."

Tugging his hand, they hurried out of the bedroom down the hall. "Where are your truck keys?"

Jericho reached for them on a small table by the door. "Cara, just slow down a second."

Cara wanted to scream at him, knowing that there was no time. Whoever was after them would not let this opportunity slip through their fingers. "We'll talk in the truck on the way to town, but right now, we need to get out!"

Jericho nodded and reached out to open the door, but it wouldn't open. Jericho tried harder, but it wouldn't budge.

"Let's try the back door."

Cara shook her head. "It's too late." Where they were standing, they could see the window in the living room. It was completely dark outside.

They moved into the living room where Jericho started to move toward his gun cabinet, but Cara stopped him.

"It won't do any good."

"If someone comes, it will help a lot!" Sadly, Cara wrapped herself against Jericho, terrified for them both. Two mortals trying to battle an immortal. It was unwinnable, they weren't going to survive.

"What she is trying to tell you is that your human weapons are useless against an immortal. Isn't that right, Cara?" Jericho felt Cara stiffen in his arms before she turned to face the woman who had appeared in the room.

"Morgana?!" Cara stared at the beautiful woman in disbelief.

"You didn't suspect me?" The woman preened at her achievement. "I worried that my spell on that stupid boy would point towards me, and certainly the magic I used in the corridor of life, but it is good to know that I covered my tracks so well."

"You didn't, I just didn't think you were powerful enough. Merlin? Yes. But you? Not in a million years."

Rage filled Morgana's face. "You dare to insult me when I hold your lives in my hands?"

"It's the truth. Pretend all you want. You may have enough power to bespell Billy, but not to enter the corridor." Morgana's lips tightened. She was about to argue further when it was as if she heard a voice in her head.

"I have been reminded that there is no time to argue with you, the eclipse will not last much longer. I must complete my task." Raising her hands and speaking in a language that Jericho didn't understand, he felt it become harder to breathe as if there were no oxygen in the room.

He tried to move forward to grab the woman, to stop whatever she was doing. As he moved forward, it was as if his body was weighted down, and his lungs were burning, starved for oxygen. He saw Cara fall to the floor, her hands at her throat.

Fury spurned him forward. When he reached her, he struck out to knock her unconscious; however she began to laugh and merely stepped away out of his reach. Jericho fell to his knees, realizing his strength was leaving. As the woman moved across the room out of his reach, he managed to crawl to Cara's side, pulling her limp body to him. His vision became blurred and he felt, more than saw, the explosion that struck the room. The room seemed to be in the center of a blaze of light that he had never experienced before. Windows burst with glass, shattering throughout the cabin, and Jericho felt oxygen slowly entering his starved lungs.

"Cara." He shook Cara, frightened more than he had ever been before. Her lids raised and relief filled him as she sat up in his tight grip.

"What happened?"

"I don't know." They both turned, hearing a woman's scream.

A huge man stood facing Morgana. He glowed, making it hard to look at him, while the darkness outside made it appear as if the sun had materialized in the room with them.

"Thor!" Morgana's triumphant expression turned to terror.

Cara and Jericho watched as Morgana raised her arms, preparing to disappear, but Thor would allow no escape. He sent a thunderbolt of electricity toward the woman and Morgana was instantly surrounded by the powerful light. Her skin and hair began to burn and smoke. Within seconds, the only thing left of the woman was a pile of ashes.

"Thor." This time it was Cara who screamed the man's name. She tore herself out of Jericho's arms and ran across the room to fling herself into the light bulb's arms. Jericho watched as Cara was gathered into the man's arms and twirled in a circle. Jericho rose to his feet, feeling like an outsider, watching their tearful reunion. Jericho should be grateful to the light bulb for saving their lives, yet he was too busy wanting to beat him for holding Cara too close.

"How did you know Morgana was here?" Cara managed to finally get the words out when he finished hugging her in his tight grip.

"I didn't. Your mother saw the eclipse coming and sent me, knowing that it would be too good an opportunity for your enemies to miss. As always, she was right." Cara didn't miss the derision that was in her brother's voice.

Cara reached up to again hug Thor. "Thank you for

saving us."

Thor looked at Jericho, not missing the jealous look on his face. "You're welcome, baby sister." Thor glanced around the small room and returned his attention to Cara. "Are you ready to return home? Your mother and family await your arrival." Cara was aware that he did not include himself in the family.

Cara smiled, anxious to see her family again, but turned to Jericho and walked back to his side.

"Tell my family that I am well, but that I cannot return." Jericho looked down at Cara as if she had lost her mind.

"No, Cara. You can't stay here. You have no hope of fighting your enemies as a human." Jericho's voice was ragged.

"I won't leave you, Jericho." Determination filled her eyes. "I can't." Jericho knew what he had to do to keep her safe.

"I want you to go." Steel entered his voice. The remoteness she was so familiar with once again entering his face and eyes. "You will only endanger me by staying. Obviously, I am not able to protect you against your family's enemy. I never gave you any hope that there was more to our relationship than sex." He hardened himself against her hurt. "Don't get us killed because you want to get laid."

Jericho looked at Thor, seeing the anger in the listening God's expression.

"Take her and go." Jericho turned to leave the room, not waiting to hear Cara's pleas.

He should have known better. He was halfway across the room when the first missile hit him in the back. He quickly turned, trying to protect himself, but it was already too late. The truck keys hit him in the face. He then saw her reaching for a bottle of water left from the poker game they had played earlier.

"That's enough, Cara." Jericho tried to make his voice

threatening. Again not a smart move. The bottle hit him in the chest.

"She's the gentle one in the family." Thor's amused voice diverted his attention long enough for Cara to grab his empty beer bottle.

Jericho realized that talking to the woman was useless, so he grabbed her before she could throw her new missile at him.

"You're a jerk. Do you know that?"

"Yes, but I'm right and you know it, Cara. I can't protect you here. It's too dangerous for you." He brushed a tear from her cheek and gave her a tender kiss on her trembling lips, trying to give her what she needed, though unable to do so. He couldn't give her a heart he didn't possess.

"I can't leave you, Jericho. I love you. Please don't ask me to leave."

Jericho turned to Thor. "Take her." He pried her hands from around his neck.

"I won't go; do you hear me, Jericho? I won't leave you." Cara screamed at Jericho's back. "Don't you dare touch me, Thor." Thor backed away from his sister, his hands raised in surrender. "I don't care if every immortal comes to take me away, or if I'm never able to see my family again. I will never leave you!"

Jericho stopped and turned back to Cara. She was on her knees on the floor, tears running down her cheeks, her body trembling. Jericho's past came to him as he stood there. For the first time in his life, he truly understood what being loved felt like. Cara loved him enough to sacrifice her life to stay with him; to give up her family and her way of life. To cry for him on her knees after all the rejection he had thrown at her. All for this, just to spend an unknown amount of time with him, a man she couldn't be sure would ever be able to return her feelings.

Something inside of Jericho broke. He felt as if the ice surrounding his soul shattered with the warmth of her love. The man he had become, unable to exist in the light of her love, suddenly was no more.

His feet slowly moved as he walked back to her. When he stood in front of her, he got down on his knees before her. His hand reached out to caress her face before raising it so that he could see her face.

"I love you," Cara whispered, brokenly. Her beautiful smile made the words that she had said over and over for the past week finally sink into his mind. She truly loved him in the purist form of the word. A love given freely without expecting anything in return other than to stay with him. To not leave him behind when it would have been easier and safer. She had done what no one else had ever done, fight for him.

He took Cara into his arms, kissing her with every ounce of emotion he had denied himself. Her arms circled his waist and held him close. A throat clearing broke the tender moment and they continued to hold each other as they turned to Thor.

Smiling, Cara looked up at her brother. "You'll be going home without me." Happiness shone from her face. Thor stared at the happy couple. "Tell my mother I love her."

"Tell her yourself." With those words, he raised his hands and sent a bolt of electricity, killing them instantly.

Thor stared at the mortal bodies lying on the floor. Sometimes, being a God just sucked.

Chapter Thirteen

"Are you still angry?" Cara murmured.

Jericho was sitting on the side of the bed with his back to her, so she scooted across the bed until she could touch him. Gently, she ran her hand down his spine. When he didn't answer, Cara moved closer until her bare breasts brushed his back. Leaning forward, she put her arms around his neck, hugging him closer to her naked body.

"Jericho?" Cara tried to keep the hurt from her voice.

"Why should I be angry? Because you're lunatic brother decided to kill us, because you could have told me you live in a palace and are practically royalty, or because your father is a *Saint*?"

Cara held him even closer. "Technically, Thor did not kill us; he just transported us to another dimension. If you had truly died on Earth, then I am sorry to say, my love, Grimm would have been your escort with a much different destination. We may live in a palace, but I would have been just as content to stay in your cabin. And you also have royal blood, being a demigod."

Cara felt his back stiffen against her and thought now might not have been the time to remind him of that fact.

When Thor had awakened them on their arrival at her mother's palace, her family had been gathered to welcome her home. Even Mother Nature and Father Time had been present, which had been a great honor.

Cara had been terrified until she had turned and seen Jericho by her side. Seeing her terror, her mother had stepped forward and explained that Thor had followed her orders, explaining that Jericho was a demigod, a human descendent of a Goddess, which explained the golden threads that Cara had seen in Jericho's soul.

Jericho had stood silently while Cara had introduced her family. Her lips twitched in a grin when she remembered Jericho's face when introduced to her father. His face had turned bright red and he hadn't looked at her father once during the dinner they sat through.

After the long dinner, Cara excused herself and Jericho, taking him to her bedroom. Before he could start with the recriminations, she had thrown herself into his arms, igniting a fire between them that lead to several hours of lovemaking.

Nibbling on his ear, Cara murmured, "My father may be a SAINT, but I'm only half. The other half is..."

The rest of her sentence was lost in a scream of surprise as Jericho turned and pulled her wiggling body onto his lap, flipping her until her stomach rested against his naked thighs.

Surprised to find herself face down across his lap, a startled cry escaped her at his first smack on her bare ass. "This is for using sex to try to manipulate me." Cara tensed her buttocks for the next smack. "Secondly, this is for not telling me about your father, and I expect you to ask him to marry us as soon as possible." This time he left his handprint on her other ass cheek. Quickly, Cara yelped her agreement.

His fingers slid between the curves of the buttocks slowly until they came to her anal canal, tracing it gently before moving on to her liquid warmth. Rubbing her wetness, his fingers parted her slit and slid deep within her tight sheath. Cara began squirming on his lap, but Jericho held her still by placing his other hand on her back. His fingers began to thrust deep within her.

Wiggling her hips, Cara began to thrust back against his fingers, trying to drive them deeper, however Jericho wasn't going to allow her any control. Removing his now slick fingers, he rubbed her clit until he felt her body stiffen in climax.

As she began to peak, his hand once again smacked her buttock. "That was for doubting that I wouldn't be as willing to sacrifice my human life as you were to sacrifice your immortal one." Still shaking from her climax, he allowed Cara to slip from his lap until she sat on the floor between his thighs. She placed a hand on each one.

"You're not angry?"

"How could I be angry to spend eternity with you?"

Smiling, Cara started giving him small kisses, alternating between each thigh. Gradually, she worked her way to his penis. Hesitantly, she reached out to touch his rigid flesh, expecting him to draw away. When he didn't, she scooted closer until she could take him in her mouth. Inexpertly, she began to suck his cock, waiting for him to tense or ask for her to stop. His hands burrowed into her long hair.

Tears silently slid down her cheeks, no words could have shown his love for her, but the trust he was now giving her spoke volumes. Her tongue swirled as she discovered his sensitive spots. His hands gripped her hair tighter when she managed to work his penis to the back of her throat while her hands stroked the long shaft she was unable to take completely into her mouth. When she felt him tense, she sucked harder until he groaned and stroked his come into her waiting throat. Cara tenderly licked his cock until Jericho's shuddering stopped. Embarrassed, Cara looked up at the man she loved to find him looking down at her.

Jericho reached down, pulling her onto his lap, kissing

each eyelid, her nose and then her swollen lips. Leaning her backwards until her breasts thrust upwards, he leaned forward and kissed the curve of each breast before placing his hand on the creamy flesh covering her heart.

"You did give me fair warning."

"I did?"

Nodding, he smiled. "When you told me you were very loveable. You were right."

"I am?" Cara was bemused by this romantic side of Jericho.

He raised his head until Cara could see clearly into his eyes. A lone tear slid free, and he didn't try to brush it away. "How could I not fall in love with you? You took my nightmares away and gave me dreams. You took my heart, but gave me yours in return." Jericho's voice grew hoarser with each word. "Do you know what I see when I look at you?'

"What?" Cara whispered.

"My love."

* * *

Fate stared at the star-filled sky, worry filling her heart for Zerina and Broni. Mixed with the worry for her daughters was the relief of having Cara home again. She was planning her next move when she felt him in the shadows of the balcony.

Pulling her shoulders back, she turned to face the consequences of her actions years ago.

"Don't leave." Her firm voice had Jericho turning back to Cara's mother.

He had gotten thirsty while waiting for Cara to wake and, not wanting to wake her, had searched for the kitchen. As he passed the balcony he had seen Fate staring pensively at the sky. He had been about to leave when she had spoken to him. He walked forward further out on the balcony until only a few inches separated them.

Fate was the most beautiful woman he had ever seen. Her gown of white hugged her body and Jericho could easily see that Cara had inherited her father's fairer looks and her mother's blue eyes.

"I'm glad we have this opportunity to speak without my daughter present."

"I don't see why, I have nothing to say that can't be said in front of Cara. I have already told Cara that I will be very happy to spend eternity with her, even though you took the choice out of our hands." Jericho turned away. "Now, if you don't mind, I was about to get a drink." His cold eyes sent chills down Fate's back.

Once again her words stopped him. "Are you going to tell her?" His eyes grew glacier, but Fate didn't back down. "You saw me that day, didn't you? You saw me and remembered me?"

"Every morning that I woke in that bitch's house, every time she touched me, I knew it was because you helped her to choose me."

"I was afraid of that. That was a disadvantage of you being a demigod; it gave you the power to see me in the room. I wasn't very happy with that, I would much have preferred that you not know. It places quite a strain on the son-in-law relationship we have in our future."

Jericho noticed it wasn't a question. She knew that he intended to marry Cara as soon as possible.

"Oh, I don't know. I'm sure I'm not the only man who hates his mother-in-law. I just have more reason than most." When Fate would have spoken he held up his hand to stop her next words. "I really don't care to hear your excuses. None of it would make the memories of her going down on me, or the men in that prison, shoving their dicks up my ass, any more bearable."

"I have no regrets about anything I have done." Jericho's hands tightened into fists at her words. Only the thought of how hurt Cara would be if she found him trying to kill her immortal mother stopped him.

"I am done with this conversation." Jericho continued to walk away; he was in the doorway when her words brought him to a halt again.

"I wasn't the one who approved her application. I was not the one who had her pick that particular adoption agency. Some things I can influence, other's only once the decisions have been made." Jericho tried to make his feet move forward, but her tormented voice held him in place.

"Should I have let her pick the little girl who the old man had plans for? She only had a few years left of her short sweet life. Her little body was already filled with an incurable disease. Should I have let her pick the little blond boy? He would have grown up so traumatized he would have become a monster himself, creating even more victims in a never-ending cycle. Instead, he grew into a doctor that will save hundreds of lives, working with children with emotional problems. The one he became the most proud of helping was a young rape victim who was unable to talk for several months. He was able to help the child regain his speech and clear an innocent man." Jericho turned in the doorway, reaching out to hold the frame.

Fate slowly walked forward until she stood before him. "Instead, I gave her a child descended from the womb of a Goddess, descended from one of the fiercest Indian chief's your world ever knew. One whose heritage is one of the most noble to ever exist. A child with a soul of a warrior.

"I saw your soul the day my eldest chose which body you would inhabit for your earthly stay and knew I would never see another with your passion to live, to… survive. I knew when that woman chose you that day what you would have to suffer, what you would have to endure, but I knew you would survive. Not whole or pure as you once were, but alive, even stronger than before because now your soul had been forged in the fires of hell.

"Yes, it was my entire fault that you were the one to suffer." Fate took a step closer to him until she was able to reach out and touch his chest where his heart laid beating. "In return, I gave you my gift. One I did not know if you would be able to treasure or abuse, even in this you did not fail. You love my daughter. I may not be the mother-in-law you want, but I chose you for Cara. No other could give her the protection, passion or love that you feel for her in your heart."

Fate's hand dropped away. Pride shown from her eyes for him that he had accepted the worst humanity had to offer, overcome every challenge, and even when hitting rock bottom with no one to depend on, had a strength that would not allow himself to be defeated. The soul of this man was worthy of her daughter.

Jericho stood speechless. All the hatred he felt for her slipped away, replaced with the love he felt for Cara. He couldn't hate her when Fate was the reason he had Cara. That terrible day she had given him to the monster had set him on a journey toward Cara. She had been responsible for the worst times of his mortal life, yet in return, she had given him an eternity filled with love.

Fate reached out and wrapped her arms around Jericho, hugging him as his mother and his adoptive mother never could have, as a son who was loved and cherished. Fate gave to him what had always been absent from his life. A mother's love.

Jericho hesitantly returned Fate's hug. "Thank you. I will cherish Cara, always."

Fate gave him a sincere smile. "I know you will." Jericho laughed at the arrogant woman, knowing if he screwed up she wouldn't hesitate to set him straight.

On the other side of the darkened doorway, Cara brushed away her tears. She didn't want Jericho to know she had been listening, but she was determined to get her fair share of the hugs before getting down to the business of bringing her sisters home. Cara wanted all her family present when she married Jericho.

Cara pasted an innocent smile on her face when she stepped out and looked away from her mother's knowing eyes to Jericho's suspicious ones and gave the pretense up. It wasn't going to be easy getting things past these two.

Sometimes, it just sucked having all these Gods around.

Epilogue

The smell of antiseptic clung to the air in the small, private room. The hospital had quieted down with the arrival of the third shift.

Edward had closed the door to give them a sense of privacy where it did not exist. Their last moments together were precious; the doctors had warned him that Mary's time was near. He sat in a chair by her bedside, holding the frail, cold hand wearing the wedding ring placed on her hand decades ago. She had been restless all evening and had slipped into a light sleep that her evening medication had produced.

"Edward." Startled Edward looked up from Mary at the gentle voice. He recognized her as the strange woman Jericho had brought to his home. Now she stood in Mary's hospital room in a flowing white gown with Jericho by her side.

Shocked to see the man who had disappeared weeks ago, Edward got to his feet.

"Jericho, where have you been? The whole town has been looking for you." As he questioned Jericho, he noticed for the first time that Jericho and Cara were both surround by a glowing light.

"Edward." Cara's soft voice once again drew his attention. "We've come for Mary." Protectively, Edward moved closer to his wife's bed.

"I don't understand. Mary is ill; she can't go anywhere with you." The sadness in their faces had Edward turning back to glance down at Mary. She was lying still in her bed, the hand in his growing colder. Tears fell down his exhausted face.

"Mary is no longer there, Edward, but with us." Edward was able to catch a glimpse of Mary's form wavering in the light beside Cara.

"Please don't take her. I can't live without her." He wasn't ashamed to beg.

Sadly, Cara shook her head and motioned to the chair by Mary's bedside. Edward didn't want to look, but felt as if he had no choice. They might leave with Mary if he didn't do as they wished. Afraid more than ever before, Edward turned to the chair and saw himself sitting there as still as Mary in her bed. His memory came back to him in a rush, remembering taking the pills. Edward had hoarded the pills carefully, and as he had watched Mary's breaths slow, he had swallowed them.

Edward saw a dark force enter the room and terror filled his soul. Exhausted as he was, words were not needed to understand who Grimm was and whose soul he was there to collect.

Cara had tried to warn him. Mary would be taken from him after all.

"Grimm, please," Cara greeted her rival, preparing herself to watch him take Edward. It would be useless to ask him to leave without the soul in which he had been dispatched to retrieve.

"Cara, it is good to see you again. Jericho." Grimm gave Jericho a curt nod.

Grimm moved towards Edward, but found his way blocked by Jericho. "Move." Grimm again moved toward

Edward's soul.

"No. You can't have him."

"You can't stop me. Cara doesn't have the power to take his soul from me. He took his own life. The consequence is inevitable. He is mine."

"Cara might not have the power, but I do." Jericho's hand reached out and took Edward's hand within his grasp and placed it within Cara's waiting one. Instantly, Edwards's soul became ethereal and floated to Mary's by Cara's side.

Grimm began to fade, becoming a dark shadow moving toward the couple now holding each other close. Jericho reached out, grabbing the shadow before he could reach his goal. At Jericho's touch, Grimm's body appeared again.

"From now on, things are going to be different." Jericho pointed towards Cara. "She gets first choice." Grimm's fury filled the room. Cara was worried; however Jericho gave her a reassuring look.

"Once dispatched, I can't return without a soul," Grimm growled out between clenched teeth. Jericho gave him a mocking smile.

"You shouldn't have to wait long; you're already in a hospital." Grimm didn't appreciate Jericho's sarcastic humor.

Grimm watched impotently as Cara and her souls moved through the waiting doorway. He just couldn't resist a parting shot. "No one takes a soul from me." Grimm gave Jericho a small warning. The last he would ever give. "You take one meant for me and then I'll take one meant for Cara."

Jericho moved before Grimm could disappear and with a hard punch to his face, sent him flying across the room where Grimm lay stunned on the floor. "Fuck with Cara, fuck with me." With a wave of his hand he had Grimm back on his feet. "You didn't lose Edward's soul to Cara; it was never meant for you. They were soul mates. Mary's love for him held him to her in life and death. Edward miscalculated that tonight wasn't Mary's time to go, but when she woke and saw what Edward had done, she quit fighting and allowed herself to die. Her love for him held her to life, prolonging her agony. Without Edward binding her soul, she was released from the unending pain. By doing so, we reached them before you could. If she had died a minute sooner or later, you would have won. Perfect timing, wouldn't you say, Grimm?" Jericho turned, walking to the doorway that Cara was waiting impatiently behind.

"What makes you think I will tolerate your interference?" Grimm was pleased he was able to get his sarcastic words passed his sore jaw.

"Fate."

Grimm's mouth dropped open in surprise. Not only was he up against Cara and her obnoxious demigod lover, but Fate had interfered. He hadn't stood a chance.

* * *

Mother Nature laughed, waking Chronas sleeping beside her. He turned, taking his wife of centuries into his arms.

"Why are you still awake?"

"Making sure Cara and Jericho return home safely."

"Have they?"

Mother Nature was silent as her mind searched outward. It didn't take her long to find her dearest friend's daughter. Images of bodies straining together, sharing their love for each other, flashed through her mind.

"Yes, they are about to create their first child." Satisfied, she laid her head on her husband's chest.

Cara and Jericho did not know that his vasectomy as a human was useless now that he was a demigod. It was going to provide her with a lot of enjoyment, watching his reaction when he found out she was pregnant. "Remind me to speak to Fate about her interference tonight." Drowsily, she was about to dose off when her husband's voice woke her.

"I thought that town was going to become a lake when you were determined that Cara stay with Jericho. That mudslide was a nice touch." Chronas reminded her of her own interference.

She shrugged in the dark, not raising her head from his warm chest. "It succeeded; he was stubborn, but not stupid. He knew a good thing when he saw it."

Her husband flipped her on her back, leaning over to give her a kiss that could still have her burning for him. "How could he resist? With you, Fate, Destiny and Rocque helping, the man did not stand a chance. Of course, now that I am awake, you can deal with me."

Mother Nature groaned as her husband began to show her exactly who had the true power.

Also by Jamie Begley

The Last Riders Series:

Razer's Ride

Viper's Run

The VIP Room Series:

Teased

The Dark Souls Series:

Soul Of A Man

About The Author

"I was born in a small town in Kentucky. My family began poor, but worked their way to owning a restaurant. My mother was one of the best cooks I have ever known, and she instilled in all her children the value of hard work, and education.

Taking after my mother, I've always love to cook, and became pretty good if I do say so myself. I love to experiment and my unfortunate family has suffered through many. They now have learned to steer clear of those dishes. I absolutely love the holidays and my family put up with my zany decorations.

For now, my days are spent at work and I write during the nights and weekends. I have two children who both graduate next year from college. My daughter does my book covers, and my son just tries not to blush when someone asks him about my books.

Currently I am writing three series of books- The Last Riders that is fairly popular, The Dark Souls series, which is not, and The VIP Room, which we will soon see. My favorite book I have written is Soul Of A Woman, which I am hoping to release during the summer of 2014. It took me two years to write, during which I lost my mother, and brother. It's a book that I truly feel captures the true depths of love a woman can hold for a man. In case you haven't figured it out yet, I am an emotional writer who wants the readers to feel the emotion of the characters they are reading. Because of this, Teased is probably the hardest thing I have written.

All my books are written for one purpose- the enjoyment others find in them, and the expectations of my fans that inspire me to give it my best. In the near future I hope to take a weekend break and visit Vegas that will hopefully be next summer. Right now I am typing away on Knox's story and looking forward to the coming holidays. Did I mention I love the holidays?"

Jamie loves receiving emails from her fans,
JamieBegley@ymail.com

Find Jamie here,
https://www.facebook.com/AuthorJamieBegley

Get the latest scoop at Jamie's official website,
JamieBegley.net

Printed in Great Britain
by Amazon